OUTPOST

A DANE MADDOCK ADVENTURE

DAVID WOOD
SEAN ELLIS

OUTPOST
Copyright 2018 by David Wood

Published by Adrenaline Press
www.adrenaline.press

Adrenaline Press is an imprint of Gryphonwood Press
www.gryphonwoodpress.com

Cover design by Matthew Williams

ISBN-13: 978-1-940095-90-5
ISBN-10: 1-940095-90-5

BOOKS and SERIES by DAVID WOOD

The Dane Maddock Adventures
Dourado
Cibola
Quest
Icefall
Buccaneer
Atlantis
Ark
Xibalba
Loch
Solomon Key

Dane and Bones Origins
Freedom
Hell Ship
Splashdown
Dead Ice
Liberty
Electra
Amber
Justice
Treasure of the Dead

Adventures from the Dane Maddock Universe
Destination-Rio
Destination-Luxor
Berserk
The Tomb
Devil's Face
Outpost

Arcanum
Magus
Brainwash
Herald
Maug
Cavern

Jade Ihara Adventures (with Sean Ellis)
Oracle
Changeling
Exile

Bones Bonebrake Adventures
Primitive
The Book of Bones
Skin and Bones
Venom

Jake Crowley Adventures (with Alan Baxter)
Blood Codex
Anubis Key

Brock Stone Adventures
Arena of Souls
Track of the Beast (forthcoming)

Myrmidon Files (with Sean Ellis)
Destiny
Mystic

Sam Aston Investigations (with Alan Baxter)
Primordial
Overlord

Stand-Alone Novels
Into the Woods (with David S. Wood)
Callsign: Queen (with Jeremy Robinson)
Dark Rite (with Alan Baxter)

David Wood writing as David Debord

The Absent Gods Trilogy
The Silver Serpent
Keeper of the Mists
The Gates of Iron

The Impostor Prince (with Ryan A. Span)
Neptune's Key
The Zombie-Driven Life
You Suck

BOOKS and SERIES by SEAN ELLIS

The Nick Kismet Adventures
The Shroud of Heaven
Into the Black
The Devil You Know (Novella)
Fortune Favors

The Adventures of Dodge Dalton
In the Shadow of Falcon's Wings
At the Outpost of Fate
On the High Road to Oblivion
Against the Fall of Eternal Night (with Kerry Frey)

The Mira Raiden Adventures
Ascendant
Descendant

Magic Mirror
The Sea Wraiths and Other Tales
Camp Zero
WarGod (with Steven Savile)

(with Jeremy Robinson)
Prime
Savage
Cannibal
Empire
Herculean
Helios
Flood Rising
Callsign: King (novella)
Callsign: King—Underworld (novella)
Callsign: King—Blackout (novella)

(with David Wood)
<u>Hell Ship</u>
Oracle
Changeling
Exile
Destiny
Mystic
Outpost
Arcanum
Magus
Destination-Rio
Destination-Luxor

PROLOGUE

The massive aircraft raced across the surface of the dark water, churning up froth and cutting a broad wake as it fought its way through the choppy waves. Dodge Dalton focused on its silver outline, his heart falling even as the plane took off and slowly gained altitude. He let out a whispered curse, watched it shrink from sight in the distance.

We've failed.

Cold wind and salty spray spattered his face, running down his cheeks in rivulets like tears, but the despair he felt was beyond sadness. He fought to suppress the images that flashed through his mind, the evils that would be unleashed. Breath came in gulps, rage ran in tremors through his body. Thousands of miles from civilization, no help coming, and nothing he could do. He felt impotent.

"There's another plane!" Hurley's cry jarred him from his reverie. He pointed at a diminutive craft floating on the swells. "It's the Duck!"

The Grumman JF "Duck" was a single-engine amphibious biplane. Compared to the massive X-314 that was even now drawing farther away, it was like a fly on an elephant's backside. But it was all they had. And though it lacked the larger craft's range, it was every bit as fast.

His heart raced. A scant hope remained.

Molly's on that plane. And the president. We have to try.

They made their way to the floating plane, steadying themselves atop its pontoons as the tiny craft rose and fell along with each cresting swell. They piled in as quickly as they dared. Dodge settled into the pilot's well while the others slid into the observer's compartment. He took a moment to familiarize himself with the controls before starting up the Wright Cyclone engine. All the while he was keenly aware that the X-314 was getting farther away with each second that passed.

The tiny plain surged forward, battered to and fro by the waves until it gained sufficient speed to take to the sky. The craft banked and yawed, the turbulent sea churning just feet beneath the tips of its wings as it teetered its way skyward. Dodge was impressed that his companions chose not to critique or react to his flying as he overcorrected several times before getting the feel of the plane.

He guided the plane upward on a steep trajectory, seeking to climb above the weather and give them a better chance of spotting their quarry. He kept the throttle wide open as he fought to gain ground on their quarry. What did it matter if he burned out the engine? If they didn't catch up with the X-314, so much more would be lost.

Hurley served as navigator, guiding them along the larger plane's path, until they finally spotted it, its running lights twinkling in the distance. For the first time since the chase had begun, he felt a glimmer of hope. Hoping luck was finally on their side, he nudged the engine a little farther into the red, gaining another five knots of speed, then turned the aircraft into a dive, gaining a couple more.

The lights grew larger and brighter. Dodge's heart leaped as the Duck ate up the intervening airspace. He glanced down at the fuel gauge. It had been at half-a-tank when they took off, and now it was down to a quarter. It was going to be a close thing. They had to close the remaining space and make their move before the engines ran dry. He resisted the urge to look down at the dark sea as he contemplated the possibility that it would be his grave.

He glanced over his shoulder toward his companions seated in the rear of the cockpit. . "When we get close enough, try to shoot out the engines. If we can force them to land, maybe we'll have a chance."

Each man replied in the affirmative. They were disciplined soldiers and would not disobey an order from their leader, no matter how mad it might sound.

The enormous flying boat seemed to materialize in front of them, a dark spot growing larger, details becoming visible. Once again he marveled at its size. It was difficult to believe that such a behemoth could even float, much less fly.

Hurley pushed the cowling back and leaned out

of one side of the plane, Hobbs the other. Dodge brought the Duck up above the Boeing and then dove, giving his companions the best possible field of fire.

Light flashed and sparks flew as the men scored hits on both starboard engines. The inner propeller continued to spin but smoke poured from the outer. Dodge brought the plane up again to assess the damage before making another attack run, but was forced to roll the plane as the Boeing's weapons returned fire.

"Damn!" He had hoped the Boeing's occupants would have taken a bit longer to register the tiny plane's presence, but no such luck. What was more, the damage they had dealt to its engine was sufficient to draw the crew's attention, but not enough to slow the plane's progress. He rolled again as another burst of fire threatened to knock them from the sky.

The Duck took a glancing hit to the fuselage, forcing Dodge to take it into a dive, and then climb again as the Boeing's gunners adjusted their fire.

"What now?" Hurley shouted.

Dodge had only one answer. The Boeing was too large, could withstand too much damage. He had to do something desperate, crazy. Heart in his throat, he shouted back to his men.

"Hang on! And be ready to move!"

He didn't add that there was a fair chance none of them would be able to move when this was over. But they had certain protections, high-tech exoskeletons, that would keep them safe.

He hoped.

Here goes nothing.

He pushed the stick forward and the tiny craft dove like a bird of prey. Closer, closer…

And then it swooped down onto the tail section of the giant X-314. The Duck's propeller blades sliced through the aluminum skin like hot knives through melted butter. With an ear-splitting shriek and a thunderous boom, the Duck smashed into the Boeing's cabin.

Dodge, he thought as the Duck's wings snapped off and its remaining fuel sprayed out onto the deck and a spark from the smoldering engine set it alight, *you'd better hope you haven't killed us all.*

CHAPTER 1

"We got a hit!"

Dane Maddock looked away from the view through the forward windscreen—a vast, limitless expanse of deep sapphire blue water, dazzling in the afternoon sun—and over to the console where his friend Corey Dean sat hunched over the display of a laptop computer. Before Maddock could ask Corey to elaborate, the imposing six-and-a-half-foot tall form of Maddock's partner and soon-to-be brother-in-law, Uriah "Bones" Bonebrake, appeared in the doorway behind him.

"Did we find it?" Bones asked, eagerly.

"Not sure what we found," Corey said, peering at the screen. "It's big."

"That's what she said," Bones quipped.

Corey studied the image a few seconds longer, then leaned back with a disappointed sigh. "But it's not big enough."

"That's what she said to Maddock," Bones said.

Maddock, who had long ago developed an immunity to his friend's off-color put downs, heard the note of disappointment in Bones' voice. "What are we looking at, Corey?"

Corey turned the screen so Maddock could see it from the helm station. The image was orange and grainy, a computer-generated visual interpretation of sound waves bouncing off the sea floor. To an untrained eye, it looked like so much static, but Maddock had seen enough side-scan sonar profiles to recognize the straight lines of a manmade object. Corey however was the expert.

"It's in several pieces. Whatever it was broke up before it reached the bottom. This largest piece is what got my attention. It's long and narrow—"

Maddock leveled a finger at Bones. "Don't say it."

Bones just kept grinning.

"I'd say about a hundred feet in length," Corey said. "The *Waratah* was five hundred feet long. There's not enough debris to indicate a ship that large."

Maddock stared at the image intently. "Judging by the shape, I'd be more inclined to say we're looking at an aircraft. Anything like that on the charts?"

"Let me check." Corey tapped in a few commands, then managed a hopeful grin. "Nope. We're the first to record anything here."

'Here' was the waters of the continental shelf about two hundred miles off the tip of South Africa. Maddock and his treasure-hunting crew—Bones and Corey, along with Willis Sanders and Matt Barnaby—were plying the waters of the southern hemisphere aboard his 80-foot motor yacht *Sea Foam*, halfway around the world from their usual stomping grounds in the Atlantic, to investigate the almost legendary disappearance of the *S.S. Waratah*.

In 1909, the *Waratah*, a five-hundred-foot-long cargo-liner with 211 passengers and crew aboard, had left Durban for Cape Town, on its way to London, and promptly vanished. Subsequent searches for the missing ship had only deepened the mystery.

Early on, it was believed that the *Waratah* was still afloat, abandoned and adrift, but extremely high seas prevented Royal Navy search vessels from entering the area where the ship was thought to be. Ten days later, the Australian government received a cable notifying them that a ship believed to be the *Waratah* had been spotted, steaming toward Durban, but that ship, whatever it was, never reached port. Three days after that, two different ships reported seeing bodies in the water near the mouth of a river two hundred miles southwest of Durban, but none were positively identified as passengers from the missing vessel. In 1912, a life-preserver with the name of the ship washed up in New Zealand, and thirteen years after that, a pilot flying over the same section of coast reported a wreck that he believed was the *Waratah*. Subsequent attempts to locate the wreck had failed to produce anything remotely definitive, but despite, or perhaps because of those failures, the quest to find the *Waratah* had taken on an almost mythic quality. Some had taken to calling it Australia's Titanic.

Maddock thought it was a fool's errand, but a wealthy action-adventure novelist with a passion for finding lost shipwrecks had come to him with a lucrative contract to conduct yet another search for the legendary vessel, this time in open water rather than along the coast where all previous expeditions had focused their attention. It was an offer Maddock couldn't reasonably refuse. Even if the search yielded no results, which was the most probable outcome, it was a valuable connection that might lead to other, more rewarding expeditions.

Now it seemed, the deal had produced some unexpected, if unrelated fruit.

"Finding the *Waratah* was always a long shot, but maybe we can solve another maritime mystery that slipped through the cracks." He pulled the throttle controls back, reversing the screws. "Might as well get some pictures before we go."

Bones grinned. "I'll get Uma prepped."

Uma was Bones' nickname for their ROV—remotely operated underwater vehicle. Although Maddock and Bones, along with their fellow crewman Willis Sanders, were all former Navy SEALs and experienced divers, there were limits to what they could accomplish with SCUBA equipment. Uma could go places that they simply could not. Places like the ocean floor nearly half-a-mile beneath *Sea Foam*'s hull.

By the time Maddock had the boat positioned above the location Corey had identified, Bones was ready to put Uma in the water. The little submersible was equipped with a high-resolution digital video camera and a powerful searchlight, but there was very little to see during the descent. The screen displaying Uma's video feed remained an unchanging black, so Maddock kept his eye on the horizon. The seas were thankfully calm, but the area they were in, at the boundary between the Indian and Atlantic Oceans, was known for rogue waves, one of which had probably been responsible for sinking the *Waratah*. Conditions under the water would be even more challenging since the collision of oceans created extraordinarily strong submerged currents. Bones was uncharacteristically subdued, focused intently on piloting Uma into the depths.

It took about fifteen minutes for the little submersible to reach the bottom and another five to locate the wreck. Maddock now turned his attention to the video screen, watching as Uma's searchlight and camera revealed the submerged landscape. The sea floor was uniformly flat and everything was a dull beige, the color of sediment. Then, with almost no warning, the wreck appeared.

"As usual, Maddock," Bones announced. "You were half-right,"

Maddock saw immediately what his friend meant. Although lightly dusted by an accretion of sediment, there was no mistaking what they were looking at: not one, but two airplane fuselages, though it was hard to tell where one ended and the other began. The aircraft were entangled like conjoined twins.

Corey shook his head in disbelief. "How did that happen?"

"Probably a mid-air collision," Maddock said. "Looks like the smaller plane almost took the tail off the bigger one."

Bones moved Uma in closer, revealing broken struts and the stubs where the wings had been sheared off. The smaller plane was about one-third the size of the other, and appeared to have been a biplane with an open cockpit. The larger aircraft actually did look more like a ship at first glance, with a wide-body that seemed better suited to riding on the high seas than cruising at high altitude, but part of one wing remained attached, complete with a single engine nacelle, sprouting three twisted propeller blades.

"Talk about a blast from the past," Corey said. "Those are vintage. How old do you think they are?"

Maddock shook his head. "Hard to say. Bones, try blowing some of that silt away. See if you can find any identifying marks."

Bones brought the ROV in even closer, until it was practically sitting in the crumpled cockpit of the smaller biplane, then turned it around and hit the thrusters, sending out a blast of water that stirred up the sediment. Uma shot away, but Bones quickly brought her back around and shone the spotlight into the cloud rising above the wreck. It only took a few minutes for the current to sweep away the sediment, revealing the instrument panel and old-fashioned stick controls. There were actually two seats in the cockpit, but both were empty. Either the crew had bailed out before the crash, or their bones had long since dissolved away.

Seeing nothing distinctive enough to make an identification of the aircraft, Bones pulled Uma back and then cautiously piloted her through the gaping hole in the top of the larger plane's fuselage.

Maddock felt a chill as the bulkheads comprising the plane's interior seemed to close around him. Unlike the cockpit of the smaller biplane, this felt much more like a place where men had died, sealed into a coffin for burial at sea. The interior reminded him a little of the cargo bay of a modern military transport plane, which perhaps contributed to his sense of foreboding. He wasn't claustrophobic, but he felt strangely anxious, and had to resist the urge to tell Bones to back away.

Uma moved down the length of the cargo bay, the camera scanning every shadowy corner for anything that might help identify the aircraft but as with the smaller plane, there were no distinguishing features.

"Might as well wrap it up," Maddock said. "We can get some more exterior shots and send them to Jimmy. Maybe he can do some computer magic and get us a positive ID."

If anyone could identify the wrecked airplanes from photographs, it was Maddock's old pal Jimmy Letson. Jimmy was both an ace investigative reporter and a computer whiz, and frequently helped Maddock out with research into subjects ranging from ancient shipwrecks to diabolical global conspiracies.

"Wait a sec," Bones said, backing Uma up and tilting her down a few degrees. "Look at that."

The image on the screen showed a misshapen triangle, made of what appeared to be black metal, lying on the deck, partly buried in silt.

"What is that?" Corey said. "A piece of the propeller?"

"It looks more like an axe head," Maddock said. "The wooden handle probably rotted away."

"Close." Bones brought the ROV in even closer until the object almost filled up the screen. "It's a tomahawk."

Maddock glanced over at his friend, skeptically. "You're sure?"

"Trust me on this, *kemosabe.*"

Maddock almost regretted having raised the question. Bones, a Cherokee Indian, was not likely to make a mistake about that.

Bones traced the outline of the object on the screen. "You can tell by the curve of the blade, and this spike on the back end. They don't really make 'em like that anymore."

"What I mean is, what's a tomahawk doing on an old airplane off the coast of South Africa?"

"Looks like there's an engraving on it," Corey said, peering at the close-up. "Can't make out what it says. A name maybe? And that looks like a date on the bottom. Nineteen-fifty-eight. Wow. You're right, Bones. That is old."

Maddock stared at the screen for a minute. "That's not a nine. It's a seven. Seventeen-fifty-eight."

Corey looked again, wide-eyed. "Holy crap."

Maddock nodded. "I think we should bring it up."

CHAPTER 2

From the comfort of his apartment in the Washington DC metro-area, Jimmy Letson watched the feed from Uma's camera. He allowed the video to play through completely before winding it back to what he thought was the best shot of the wrecked airplanes and froze the playback there. With a couple of mouse-clicks he was easily able to isolate the airframe and create a three-dimensional model, which he then compared against the Jane's aircraft identification database.

"Easy peasy," he announced just thirty seconds later. "Your wreck is a Boeing 314, sometimes called a Clipper."

It took a few seconds for the Skype transmission to bounce through Jimmy's extensive proxy-chain network to reach Maddock's computer on the far side of the world, and then for Maddock's reply to return. "Clipper? One of the old flying boats from the 1930's?"

"Like the plane in *Raiders of the Lost Ark*?" Bones chimed in. "The red line express."

Jimmy grinned. "Right. Although that scene is a bit anachronistic. The 314 wasn't produced until 1938, which was two years after Raiders supposedly took place."

"What can you tell us about this specific plane?"

Maddock asked.

"Without tail numbers or some other identifier, not much." Jimmy tapped in a few keystrokes. "Oh. That's strange." He reread the data on the screen, wondering if he had overlooked something.

"What's strange?"

"Well, it turns out that only twelve Clippers were ever produced, which would ordinarily make this a pretty simple process of elimination. But it looks like all twelve are accounted for. Only two of them crashed—neither one anywhere close to where you are—and both were scuttled in place. All the rest were scrapped for parts."

"Could those records be wrong?"

"Possibly," Jimmy admitted. "The Clipper fleet was pressed into war time service. Maybe one of the planes was requisitioned for a secret mission and to cover it up, they listed it as scrapped. I'll have to do a little more digging into that."

"What about the smaller plane?"

"Not enough left of it for me to work my magic. I'm good, but not that good."

"Sounds like he's holding out on us," Bones said after a moment.

"I wish I were," Jimmy said. "But even if I could narrow it down to a specific airframe design, we'd still be looking at hundreds of possibilities, and unlike a big passenger plane, a lot of those old biplanes ended up in private hands. Some are probably still flying today."

"Fair enough," Maddock said. "Okay, switching

gears. I'm sending you pics of the tomahawk we found."

While he waited for the image file to arrive, Jimmy played with various search strings that included terms like: Clipper; Africa; crash; missing. One of the crashed 314's had been originally called the *Cape Town Clipper*, but its demise had occurred off the coast of Portugal, thousands of miles from where Maddock had discovered the sunken aircraft. After a few minutes, he tabled the effort. Identifying the wreck was going to take some real digging which oddly pleased him. He liked a challenge.

A chime sounded to alert him to the arrival of a file attachment. He opened it and saw a photograph of an axe head with a sharp spike on the back end. The metal was dark, almost black, without any signs of corrosion. A second photograph was a close-up of the engraving on the flared blade.

Steven Thorne
28, April 1758

"President Monroe was born that day," Maddock supplied. "I doubt that's relevant."

Jimmy knew that Maddock wouldn't have enlisted his help without first trying his own hand at the Google game, but Maddock wasn't a professional researcher. "That would have been smack in the middle of the French and Indian War. Tomahawks were issued to colonial militia. They weren't just used by Indians, you know."

"No kidding," Bones rumbled, with just a hint of sarcasm. "So that Mel Gibson movie wasn't total crap after all?"

Jimmy let the comment slide. "I'd guess this Thorne was a militia officer. There are records of that stuff believe it or not, but most of them haven't been digitized."

"Our working theory is that the tomahawk was a family heirloom that belonged to a member of the plane's crew," Maddock said. "One of Steven Thorne's descendants. If you can trace his genealogy, we might be able to figure out who it was, and from there, figure out what he was doing on that plane."

"Not bad, Maddock. I can definitely try that." Jimmy scrolled through the results of his cursory search. "Thorne was already a very common surname in colonial America. Particularly in New York." He drummed his fingers on the desktop. "I might be able to whittle the list down a bit, but I'm limited to what's actually been put into the online databases, and that may only be a fraction of what's available. Your best bet would be to talk to a historian, someone who specializes in the colonial period. Show them that tomahawk, and they'll probably talk your ear off."

The silence went on too long to merely be the result of signal lag. Maddock had clearly and simply hit the disconnect button, eager to get started on what had the makings of an honest-to-goodness historical mystery.

There were, as he saw it, three possible solutions.

The first, was that his preliminary identification might have been wrong. He had initially rejected that possibility since there were no other planes that matched both the dimensions and shape of the airframe. The closest similar aircraft, the Martin M-130, had a similar profile, but was nearly twenty feet shorter than the Boeing 314. As aviation technology improved during the war years, the need for large aircraft with water-landing abilities diminished, and designers began favoring a more streamlined cylindrical fuselage design, as compared to the Clipper, which was almost square in profile.

The second possible solution—and the likeliest—was what he had suggested to Maddock: an error—intentional or accidental—in the historical record. He started by verifying the accuracy of reports concerning the fate of the twelve Clippers, which he was able to do up to a point. The records did exist, but not in such detail that he could rule out a falsification or cover-up. When he felt he had exhausted that line of research, he turned to the third possibility: the existence of an unrecorded thirteenth Clipper.

Figuring he could kill two birds with one stone, he surreptitiously probed—Maddock would have said 'hacked,' but Jimmy disliked the term—Boeing's archives looking for more detailed records of the 314 aircraft project. He spent a good half-hour browsing the logs of the twelve known aircraft, before expanding the search parameters to look for unlucky number thirteen. He noted that the Clipper tail numbers ranged from NC18601 to NC18612, with three exceptions—the seventh, eighth and tenth planes—had been sold to Great Britain and issued new tail numbers. On a whim, he tried looking for NC18613, and then NC18600, but neither search yielded anything meaningful. He tried several different approaches to no better effect, before deciding to take a break from the search. There were other avenues available to him. If nothing else panned out, he could probably find some answers, or at least some better questions, on an aircraft history forum. He clicked on the X to close the browser window and stood up to stretch his legs.

When he looked down again, he saw that the browser was still open. Frowning, he moved the cursor over the X again, and clicked on it, but the screen refused to wink out. He tried the shortcut keys, and saw a message appear on the header: (Not responding).

Jimmy Letson felt a sudden chill. He quickly entered the shortcut to bring up the task manager, but the computer seemed to be ignoring him.

To an ordinary computer user, that would be an annoyance, but to Jimmy, it felt like staring into the abyss.

Somebody had taken note of his intrusion.

"Not possible," he whispered. But what other

explanation could there be?

Without a moment's hesitation, he threw the master power switch, killing the flow of electricity not only to the computer, but also to the network of router-repeaters he used to hide his physical location from the World Wide Web.

The risk of getting caught had long ago ceased to be a source of thrills for Jimmy. He kept his hacks very low profile, and utilized redundant proxy chains to reduce the chances of anyone back-tracing his IP address. The repeater network, which stretched across two suburban Virginia neighborhoods, was his last line of defense—removing him from the physical location associated with the IP address. That system was bombproof, he was sure of it….

Mostly sure of it.

He waited ninety seconds before restoring power and booting up the system, one subroutine at a time, running diagnostics as he went to see if anything had been compromised. Lastly, he started up the repeater network and accessed the Web.

Despite the fact that he kept his apartment a mild sixty-eight degrees, Jimmy was sweating. "It's nothing," he told himself. "You're just jumping at shadows, ace."

He brought up the connection logs for the chain of IP proxy servers, but that was as far as he got. When he tried to edit the logs, he received an error message informing him to contact the system administrator.

"Locked out," he whispered.

He hit the power switch again and stood up quickly, backing away from the computer as if it were red hot.

Hollywood depictions notwithstanding, tracing someone's IP address, particularly when the connection was routed through multiple international proxies, was a challenging and time-consuming process. The fact that someone had blocked his access to the connection logs of servers in six different countries, to effectively prevent him from wiping away his digital fingerprints, indicated that he had just woken up one hell of a big sleeping giant.

He couldn't erase the source IP address, that much was certain. The unknown hunter would trace it back to a trendy coffee shop that Jimmy had never once visited, and that would be the end of that, provided he never tried logging in with that IP address ever again.

At least he hoped that was the case.

What if they find the repeaters?

He shook his head. No. He was a needle in a haystack. As long as he kept his head down, he would be fine.

But maybe it was time for a nice vacation. A road trip.

As he headed out the door, he wondered exactly what it was he had blundered into. He couldn't believe that an eighty-year old plane crash was a secret big enough to necessitate such a swift and decisive response, but what other explanation was there?

He would have to get word to Maddock somehow. Warn him to back off, lay low.

If it wasn't already too late.

CHAPTER 3

Maddock glanced over his shoulder, taking one last look at Durban harbor, and then steered *Sea Foam* south, toward the search area. With its sub-tropical climate, palm trees and festive, touristy vibe, Durban, South Africa reminded him a lot of Miami, South Beach, and that made him think about Key West, which in turn made him homesick. It was a new feeling for him, and probably had something to do with the fact that, for the first time in a long time, there was somebody waiting at home for him.

Well, not literally.

Angelica Bonebrake, a professional mixed-martial-arts fighter, was training for an upcoming championship bout, and that left her with little time—or energy—for domestic pursuits. That was fine with Maddock. They were both independent people with careers that meant a great deal to them, and were more than comfortable with the idea that there would be times when they wouldn't see a lot of each other.

Still, he was a bit surprised at how much he missed her, and felt the mildest twinge of jealousy toward Bones and Willis who were probably somewhere over the Atlantic, on their way back to the States to follow up on the tomahawk head, while he was stuck with what he knew in his gut would be a fruitless search for a ship that refused to be found. Normally, that wouldn't have bothered him. He liked being on the water, liked looking for things that had eluded everyone else, but right now, the mystery that was calling to him was not the *Waratah*, but Steven Thorne's pre-Revolutionary War axe and the as-yet-unidentified plane wreck where it had evidently spent the better part of a century. Unfortunately, he was the boss, and that meant he had to stay focused on the job at hand, running grids until he could say with certainty where the *Waratah* wasn't. Besides, Bones was probably better suited to chasing the mystery of the tomahawk than he was, and since they couldn't both leave the operation, Willis was the logical choice to accompany Bones and keep him out of trouble, which even Bones would admit was probably a good idea.

He was also disappointed that Jimmy had not gotten back to him. Usually, he could count on his old friend coming up with answers to the stickiest research questions in a matter of hours, if not mere minutes, but it had been twelve hours since Jimmy ended the Skype call, and in that time Maddock had not heard a peep from the hacker.

Maybe he had finally handed Jimmy a nut that couldn't be cracked.

The answer, whatever it was, would probably have to wait a few more days. While Maddock had a satellite phone, capable of both voice and data transmissions, satellite coverage in the region was iffy at best, which was the primary reason why they had been obliged to make the unscheduled port call.

Quit stalling, he told himself. *Time to get back to work.*

Maddock and his two remaining crew members—Corey and Matt Barnaby—took turns at the helm for the ten-hour cruise back to the search area. It was just after midnight when they reached their destination, but since they didn't need daylight to look for shipwrecks on the sea floor, they immediately deployed the sonar "fish" and started down the next lane on the search grid at a sedate twelve knots. Maddock knew that the lane would eventually bring them close to the spot where they had found the crashed planes and expected to find more debris, but that wouldn't happen for at least a couple hours. What he did not expect however was a radar contact on the surface.

"Where did he come from?" Corey asked.

Maddock eyed the orange blob on the radar display. It had appeared suddenly, blinking into existence seemingly from out of nowhere. The signature was too well-defined to be a cloud and too small to be a rogue wave. It had to be another vessel, and it was coming after them at a speed of about twenty-five knots.

"We're outside the shipping lanes," Corey said. "What's he doing out here?"

Maddock could think of only one answer. "He's

looking for us."

He grabbed a pair of binoculars and headed out onto the open deck, but all he could see through the high-powered glasses was inky blackness. The approaching vessel was running dark.

"Corey," he called out, still sweeping the horizon with the binoculars. "Bring in the fish." Then he added, "Matt, prepare to repel boarders."

Corey poked his head out from the bridge. "Seriously?"

"Seriously," Maddock said. "Pull in the fish."

"I meant the other part. Repel boarders?"

"Let's hope it doesn't come to that," Maddock said, but he knew hope alone wouldn't do the trick. While he couldn't begin to guess at their motive, there was little question in his mind that the other vessel had hostile intentions.

While Corey reeled in the towed sonar array, Matt—a former-Army Ranger—broke out their arsenal, which consisted of a single AR-15 and two semi-automatic pistols: a Colt M1911 and Maddock's favorite, a Walther P99. He handed Maddock the latter, and kept the other two weapons for himself.

"So what are we dealing with? Pirates?"

"Your guess is as good as mine, but I'd rather not wait around to ask them in person." Maddock stuffed the gun in his waistband and passed the binoculars to Matt. "They're coming in from our four o'clock. I'll try to outrun them."

Matt took the glasses and started scanning the

water to starboard while Maddock returned to the helm station. The radar screen showed the approaching vessel was less than two nautical miles away from them and still closing fast. As soon as Corey gave the signal, Maddock pushed the throttles to full.

They immediately pulled away from the pursuer, but within minutes, the gap was shrinking again. The skipper of the other boat had somehow found a way to wring another five knots out of his craft, which was just a little faster than *Sea Foam*'s maximum cruising speed.

Maddock considered his options. If he redlined *Sea Foam*'s engines, he might be able to squeeze a little more speed from them, but at the risk of doing permanent damage and even then, there was no guarantee that they would be able to elude the hunters. In fact, it was far more likely that they would blow a gasket or throw a screw long before reaching safe harbor, at which point they would be completely at the mercy of the pursuer.

If he didn't, the other ship would overtake them within the hour. Sooner or later, the hunters would catch up to them.

Maddock reached for the throttle, but instead of pushing it forward, he drew it back all the way.

Full stop.

Matt stuck his head in a few seconds later. "What's wrong?"

"You know that old saying about the best

defense being a good offense? We're about to put it to the test."

CHAPTER 4

As soon as he was out of the cab and standing on the sidewalk, Bones hugged his arms across his chest and grimaced. "Frigging Maddock."

Willis looked back at him. "What are you whining about now?"

"'I should stay with the boat,'" Bones said, in a mocking falsetto. "'Bones, you're the adventurous one. You should go.' You think he didn't know it was below freezing here?"

Willis shook his head. "Man, first of all, it was your idea to come here…" He took out his phone and tapped the screen a couple times to bring up a local weather report. "Where it's actually forty-one degrees, which ain't below freezing. Second…that's about the worst Maddock impersonation I've ever heard."

Bones rolled his eyes. "Kiss ass. Where else were we going to go to do research on an artifact from the French and Indian War? Honolulu?"

"Fine. Let's get inside. I know how sensitive you are to cold temperatures."

"What the hell is that supposed to mean? And don't say a thing about shrinkage."

Willis just grinned and started up the walk to the front doors of Park Hall, where the History Department of University at Buffalo was located.

Despite Bones' comment, they had not come to the upstate New York locale simply because of its proximity to the battlefields of a war that was even older than America. During the long flight from South Africa, Bones had put in a call to Avery Halsey. Avery was Maddock's half-sister and Bones' ex-girlfriend—one of many—and worked for a special CIA task force, which he and Maddock sometimes moonlighted for, but before she had taken that job, she had been a college history professor. Avery didn't have any particular insights for them, but she had recommended a colleague, and arranged a meeting for them.

As they entered the History Department offices on the fifth floor, Bones spied an attractive red-haired thirty-something woman behind the reception counter. He stepped forward quickly to beat Willis to the introduction. "Hi," he said, leaning one elbow and the counter, which brought him down to her eye-level. "I came here to see Dr. Greer, but it looks like I saw you first."

The woman burst out laughing. "Oh my goodness. Does that line ever work for you?"

Bones grinned. "You tell me. No, wait. How about you tell me tomorrow, after breakfast. I'm from out of town, so…your place?"

The woman was still laughing, but the twinkle in her hazel eyes told Bones that she wasn't laughing at him. Not too much, anyway. "Well, that's quite an offer," she said. "But I think you skipped a couple meals. I haven't even had lunch yet."

"Great. Me either. Let's go."

The woman grinned. "Tempting. I was supposed to be meeting someone here to talk about some boring old history, but hey…why not?"

Willis finally broke his silence. "You wouldn't happen to be Dr. Greer, by any chance?"

"My students call me Dr. Greer," she replied, turning her warm and slightly mischievous smile in his direction. "You can call me Rose." She glanced back at Bones. "If you behave, you can, too."

"When you say behave…?"

Rose shook her head in mock-despair. "My goodness. Avery wasn't kidding about you."

Bones winced. Even though his post-relationship-relationship with Avery Halsey was amicable, she was still an ex. There was no telling what she had done to poison the well.

"All kidding aside…" He slid his backpack off his shoulder and took out a cloth-wrapped bundle. "We should probably get down to business."

Rose's eyes flashed with anticipation, but she shook her head. "Let's do this in my office." She came around the counter and led them down a short hall to a small perfunctory room with an uncluttered desk and a row of utilitarian plastic chairs against one wall.

"This is your office?" Bones remarked. "I would have expected a history professor to have more… stuff."

Rose shrugged. "I keep my stuff elsewhere. This is mostly just a place for advisory meetings." She gestured to the desk. "Well, let's see it."

Bones set down the bundle and unwrapped it to reveal the axe head. Rose's forehead immediately creased into a frown. "Is this a joke?" Her voice had gone several degrees colder than the air outside.

Willis came forward. "If so, the joke's on us, ma'am. Is there a problem?"

"It's widely known that I'm looking for the hatchet that belonged to Captain Steven Thorne. I've seen plenty of decent fakes, but that looks like something you picked up from a hardware store on the drive over."

"I can assure you, it's not," Willis said. "I can't speak to its authenticity, but we found it in a sunken aircraft. At the very least, it's nearly a century old."

"Sunken aircraft?" Rose looked up suddenly, her eyes widening in surprise for a moment. Then she shook her head again. "No, I'm sorry. I simply don't believe you." She held her hand over the axe head, but seemed reluctant to touch it. "You can't actually expect me to believe that this has been immersed in water for decades."

Bones shrugged. "Believe what you want. If you aren't interested, maybe you can recommend someone who might be."

Willis held up his hands. "Let's all just take a step back, okay? You'll have to pardon us ma'am. We're a bit jet lagged. I promise you, we're not trying to shine you on. This is what we found, but we don't understand what it means. Or how it ended up where it did. We were hoping you could shed some light on that."

The historian drew her hand back, folded her arms across her chest in what might have been a defiant pose, but then just as quickly reached out for the tomahawk blade and picked it up. She tilted it so the overhead light was shining on the engraving. "Steven Thorne was an officer in a colonial militia company. Rogers Rangers."

Bones and Willis exchanged a grin. "Ma'am, we're former military," Willis explained. "We both attended Ranger school. They made us memorize Rogers' Rules. Rule number two: 'Have your musket clean as a whistle, hatchet scoured.' Some Ranger units still carry tomahawks to this day."

Bones added, "My favorite was always: 'Let the enemy come till he's almost close enough to touch, then let him have it and jump out and finish him up with your hatchet.'"

Rose smiled despite herself. "I'm afraid your instructors did you a disservice. Those 'rules' were actually adapted from the novel *Northwest Passage*, written in 1937. I'm afraid Major Robert Rogers' actual Rules of Ranging are quite a bit more prosaic, but you are correct about the importance of the hatchet." She glanced at Bones. "Or tomahawk, if you prefer.

"Captain Thorne fought with the Rangers during the French and Indian War, and probably carried several hatchets over the years, but according to family legend, he passed one down to his son, who carried it during the Revolutionary War. It was handed down through the family for several generations, and through several wars."

Bones and Willis exchanged another look. "One of Thorne's descendants was on that plane," Willis said. "We figured it had to be something like that. What we don't have is a name."

Rose frowned again. "You say you found this in a wrecked plane? Underwater?"

Bones nodded. "A couple hundred miles off the coast of South Africa. The plane was one of the old Clippers from the 1930s but we haven't been able to find a record of a crash."

Rose pursed her lips together as if still trying to make up her mind about her visitors, then took a deep breath. "In 1867, the wife of Colonel Zane Thorne—a veteran of the Civil War—gave birth to a daughter—their only child, whom they named Rosalyn. Rosalyn was a bit of a tomboy, and while she couldn't carry on the family tradition of military service, she did earn quite a name for herself as a war reporter for a New York newspaper. I've always entertained the notion that she carried the old Ranger hatchet with her on her adventures, but if she did, she didn't advertise the fact.

"Rosalyn Thorne eventually married a man named Jack Falcon—actually, he was born Giacomo Falcone, but he Americanized it before he and Rosalyn married. Their son, Zane Falcon, carried the hatchet with him during World War I, where he commanded an infantry company. As far as we know, he was the last member of the Thorne family to hold it."

"Did he die in the war?" Willis asked.

"No." Rose sounded less than certain. "What became of Captain Zane Falcon after the war is a matter of some debate. It's difficult to separate fact from fiction."

Bones immediately recognized the name. "Wait. Captain Falcon was a real dude?"

Willis now fixed Bones' with a questioning stare. "You've heard of this guy?"

"Yeah. I mean, sort of. He was a character in some of those old adventure pulp novels."

Willis just blinked at him, uncomprehending.

"You know, like Doc Savage or Brock Stone?"

Willis shook his head. "Sorry. Never heard of any of those guys. Pro wrestlers?"

"Jeez, did you grow up under a rock?" He turned to Rose. "When I was a kid, my uncle—Crazy Charlie—had a big box of them in the garage. Captain Falcon. Hurricane Hurley. The Padre… Oh, man. What a blast from the past. I devoured those things. And he was a real guy?"

Rose inclined her head slightly. "Just like Buffalo Bill Cody or Wild Bill Hickok—actual historical figures whose exploits were exaggerated and fictionalized in the dime novels. It's unlikely that any of the stories of Captain Falcon's adventures are true, but yes… he was a real person. And this isn't the first time someone has 'found' Captain Falcon's legendary hatchet."

Bones looked at her sideways. "Rose…Rosalyn. That's not a coincidence, is it? You're family?"

"Actually, it is a coincidence. No relation, at least none that I'm aware of. Rose was my great-grandmother's middle name. That particular branch of the Thorne family tree died with Captain Falcon."

"How did he die?" Willis asked.

Rose drew in another breath. "As I said, it's always been rather difficult to separate fact from fancy when it comes to Captain Falcon. My great-grandfather wrote those stories believing it was all a fiction. It was only later that he learned the truth. Or what he believed was the truth."

"Wait, Dodge Dalton was your great-grandfather?" Bones turned to Willis. "That's the guy who wrote the Captain Falcon stories."

"Great-grandad Dodge wrote a story he claimed was a true account of his search for the real Captain Falcon." She hesitated a moment. "That book, *In the Shadow of Falcon's Wings*, ends with Falcon's death. Aboard a plane that crashed into the sea after leaving Antarctica."

"Antarctica?" Willis shook his head. "That's at least two thousand miles from where we found the wreck."

"The aircraft in the story was a prototype for a long range seaplane. Would that match your wreck?"

Before Bones could answer in the affirmative, he

saw Rose's gaze suddenly shift to the door behind them. He turned, curious to see what had distracted her, just as the grenade came flying into the office.

CHAPTER 5

The assault team leader grinned as he saw a hot white plume rising from the target vessel. The eighty-foot motor yacht, was still a good half-mile away, too far out for him to see the crew, even with his enhanced night-vision goggles, but the smoke was impossible to miss.

"Well that explains why they're slowing," he said into the throat mic of his Motorola tactical radio. "Looks like they blew an engine. Stay frosty, gents. They know we're coming, and if they're armed, we can expect a warm welcome."

The five shooters acknowledged with mumbled affirmatives. They were already hunkered down behind the gunwales of the sixty-five-foot cabin cruiser, weapons cocked, locked and ready to rock at the first sign of incoming fire.

The leader would have preferred to simply drill the boat full of holes from a distance, but his handler had promised a bonus if they recovered any useful material—computers, written notes and photographs, artifacts—and that would be a whole lot harder to do if the motor yacht was shot all to hell.

He secretly hoped the other crew would surrender without a fight. That would certainly make killing them a lot easier.

He waited until they had closed to within a hundred yards of the drifting yacht before giving the order to back off the throttles. A haze of smoke hung over the other vessel, and the salt air was tinged with the odor of burning oil, but there was no sign of activity aboard.

The assault team leader didn't like that one bit. "Anyone got eyes on?" he said, subvocalizing into the mic.

The replies came back one at a time—all negative.

His 2IC—second-in-command—who was standing beside him, manning the auxiliary helm on the flying bridge, wrapped it up succinctly. "They're either hiding below decks or they bugged out."

The leader's instincts told him the other crew was still on the target vessel, but he had to consider all the possibilities. "I don't see their dinghy. Could we have missed them taking off?"

"We would have seen the heat from an outboard on IR."

"Not if they were rowing."

The 2IC shrugged in the darkness.

"Okay, let's assume they're still there, waiting to jump out when we try to board. I want you covering the hatches from here while we go over tactically, and clear the objective top down."

"Shouldn't we fire a shot across their bow? Give 'em a chance to surrender?"

"Nah. Why waste a bullet?" The leader keyed his mic again. "Go on my signal. And if you see anything moving, shoot to kill."

The jolt that vibrated through the hull as the blacked-out pursuit boat bumped up against *Sea Foam*, was Maddock's signal to move. He gave Corey's shoulder a reassuring squeeze, then dipped his head below the black water, and began moving his legs in a powerful scissors-kick. The long diving-flippers on his feet supplied extra energy to each kick, allowing him to move through the water with a minimum of effort, and more importantly, without creating a disturbance that might be visible to anyone on the other boat looking for him.

Reasoning that the attackers would have superior numbers, Maddock had made the decision to avoid a head-on confrontation. After setting a small oil fire on the deck near the engine hatch to simulate a breakdown, he and Corey—the only member of his crew with no military experience—had gone into the water on the sheltered side of the boat. Matt Barnaby would remain aboard to 'greet' the boarding party.

Maddock kept one hand extended out before him, maintaining contact with *Sea Foam*'s hull until he reached the waterline. Although he couldn't see a thing, he knew the other boat was there, right in front of him, and that if he wasn't careful, he might smack his head against the hull. Even if the impact didn't knock him unconscious, it would almost certainly reveal his presence to the crew, taking away his one advantage: the element of surprise.

He groped forward with both hands until his fingers encountered something solid—the hull of the second boat. He rested his fingers against it, feeling faint vibrations as the vessel rocked gently in the calm seas. High above, he knew, the boarding party was crossing over to seize their prize.

He was running out of time.

He kicked forward again, swimming fast but smooth, until he reached the far side of the boat. He surfaced quietly near the bow, then worked his way down its length to the stern. Although the sky was overcast, hiding moon and stars, the darkness on the surface was by no means absolute. A stripe of faint blue-green lit up the water near the aft-end of the boat—bioluminescent plankton stirred up by the churning screws—and a silvery haze smudged the sky, marking the moon's location in the heavens. It was just enough to reveal the silhouette of the boat above him.

Moving slow and stealthy in order to avoid literally rocking the boat, he crawled up onto the swim platform where he slipped off his flippers and took his Walther from the ZipLoc bag he'd used to keep it dry. He was just about to check the luminous dial of his watch to see how much time he had left when he heard the pop and hiss of an Orion Starblazer aerial signal flare shooting five hundred feet up into the sky.

Maddock kept his head down, eyes averted from

the tiny red sun that blossomed into existence high overhead.

Perfect timing, Corey. Maddock thought as he rolled over the transom.

He knew the flare would only last a few seconds, but while it burned, it would level the playing field a little and if the attackers were using some kind of night-vision tech, as he was almost certain they were, then it might just give him an advantage. Bright light could temporarily disable night observations devices—NODs—or even briefly blind a man wearing them.

Maddock swept the pistol back and forth, searching the rear deck for targets, but there was no one there. The bad guys were all evidently on *Sea Foam*.

He kept moving, running for the ladder-like steps up to the flying bridge, then bounding up them. As his head cleared the deck, he spied someone at the helm controls. The man was little more than a shadow, outlined in red. He wore black tactical gear, his face hidden by a matching balaclava and a set of NODs, which he was evidently trying to reset. His head snapped toward Maddock and his hands dropped to the pistol holstered at his belt.

That was when the flare went out, plunging the world once more into darkness.

Maddock fired once, the muzzle flash revealing that his target had already moved, then shifted his aimpoint and fired two more shots.

The night erupted in gunfire.

Maddock leapt up onto the flying bridge and threw himself flat on the deck. He was pretty sure he'd hit the man with both shots; if he hadn't, he would know pretty soon. In any case, the shooting was all coming from *Sea Foam*; evidently, the boarding party had met a little resistance.

Keep your head down, Matt.

He groped forward until his hands encountered the unmoving form of the man he'd just shot. His fingers slid across familiar textures—Nomex and nylon webbing, similar to gear he had worn on SEAL missions. The man wore a tactical vest, festooned with pouches for magazines, grenades and other gear. Maddock kept going until his hands found what he was really after: the man's NODs.

He wrestled them off the man's head and held them up to his own eye, working the power button to turn them on.

Aside from a faint streak across the display—the after-image of the flare—the world was revealed in glorious green-tinged monochrome. The first thing he saw was the would-be attacker lying supine on the deck in front of him. The man was still alive, stirring and groaning in pain as he struggled to stay conscious. Maddock's aim had been dead-on, but his opponent's tactical vest was more than just a place to store extra gear. It had Kevlar inserts and plate hanger, both of which had stopped the rounds from the Walther cold.

The man's eyes flashed open, his pupils already dilating to adjust for the darkness. In the display of the NODs they looked like the glowing orbs of some supernatural entity.

He can't see me, Maddock thought.

Then the man's hands shot out and closed around his neck.

Maddock reflexively tried to pry the fingers loose, dropping both the NODs and his Walther in the process. That was about all he accomplished. The man's stranglehold felt like an iron band across his throat. He could feel his pulse throbbing, his blood forcibly dammed before it could deliver life-sustaining oxygen to his brain. Through the fog, he could hear the man shouting, calling out to his comrades for assistance.

Maddock knew he would not be able to break the man's grip, not in the second or two left before he lost consciousness, so he pushed back the primal impulse to struggle, and instead met the problem head-on. He reached out and grabbed the man's head in both hands and smashed his forehead into the bridge of the man's nose.

The impact sent a flash of pain through Maddock's skull, and the sound of cartilage snapping reverberated through his cranium, but mercifully, the stranglehold slackened enough for him to squirm free. He thrust the man away from him, slamming his head into the deck until the man stopped struggling.

As the fog lifted, Maddock heard answering shouts from below. At least some of the boarding party were crossing back to their vessel in response to the calls for help. He had no idea how many he would be facing, but knew that his Walther wouldn't be enough to stop them, especially if they were all wearing body armor.

He needed something a lot more powerful.

Groping in the darkness, he quickly found the stunned man's tactical vest, tore open one of the pouches and pulled out a baseball-sized object. Muscle memory took over from there. He deftly stripped off the metal safety band, slipped a finger through the split-ring dangling from the arming pin, yanked it out, and then, with an almost indifferent flick of his hand, he tossed the fragmentation grenade out onto the rear deck of the cabin cruiser.

As soon as the grenade left his hand, Maddock dove over the control console and slid down the sloped superstructure onto the foredeck. In the faint light, he could make out a human form moving right in front of him. There was a shout, and then a muzzle flash as the man started shooting. The air around Maddock sizzled with incoming rounds, the Plexiglas window cracking with multiple impacts. Maddock kept moving, rolling toward the shooter, praying the grenade would detonate before the gunman got a bead on him. He figured the superstructure would shield them both from the blast and the deadly spray of hot metal, but hopefully the explosion would distract the man long enough for him to—

There was a flash, and then he was weightless and spiraling down into the darkness.

CHAPTER 6

The flash-bang grenade was small and cylindrical, its highly reactive magnesium core partially shielded by a heavy-duty aluminum shell that was perforated with holes like a piece of Swiss cheese. Bones instantly recognized it as it sailed through the air toward them. Before it could hit the floor, he turned away and dove across the desk, tackling Rose to the ground behind it. The desk would shield them from the one million candle-power magnesium flash, but there wasn't much he could do about the bang except tilt his head to the right, partially covering his ear with a shrugged shoulder. The standard stun grenade produced 180 decibels of sound, a noise louder than a jet engine or a shotgun blast.

In the confined space of the small office, it hit like a sledge-hammer.

Bones' bell had been rung by flash-bangs plenty of times during SEAL training exercises, and he knew how to cope with the disorienting aftermath, but that didn't make it any less unpleasant. A loud whining sound, like the noise of a hospital EKG flatlining, pierced through Bones' skull. He felt like he was on a spinning merry-go-round, unable to tell which way was up, and knew that if he tried to stand, he would immediately crash sideways.

He knew what he would not be able to do, but

he also knew what he still could do.

Twisting around, he got his hands on the edges of the desktop, and then without rising, started pushing, shoving the desk across the room.

He got only a few feet before the desk struck something. The sudden jolt caused Bones to slip and fall forward, but as his face hit the floor, he glimpsed a pair of shoes protruding through the narrow gap at the bottom of the desk.

That explained the abrupt stop. He had just run into someone.

They weren't Willis' shoes, so Bones figured they had to belong to the same person who had tossed the flash-bang into the room.

Bones scrambled forward again, thrusting head and shoulders into the kneehole beneath the desk, and then stood up, erupting off the floor like a jack-in-the-box, heaving the desk forward as he did.

The desk tilted away, the top slamming the unseen attacker backward, but because Bones was still woozy from the flashbang, he reeled sideways and crashed onto the overturned desk. There was a stabbing pain in his chest as he struck its underside. That discomfort would be nothing compared to what a bullet might do if he didn't keep moving, but he allowed himself a triumphant smile as he spotted the shoes again, now protruding from under the desk like the legs of the Wicked Witch of the East sticking out from under Dorothy's house. It was too soon to declare victory though. Bad guys, like Wicked Witches, usually had back-up.

The air in the office was thick with smoke, but through the haze, Bones saw Willis darting toward him, evidently a lot more steady on his feet than Bones was. Willis knelt and scooped up a pistol, outfitted with a sound suppressor, and aimed it toward the door.

It took Bones a few seconds to register the fact that Willis was shouting at him. He still couldn't hear a thing, but when Willis pointed back at Rose, he was able to make a rough guess.

Get the girl.

Something like that anyway.

Bones rolled off the desk, but stayed on hands and knees, unsure of his equilibrium. He reached Rose a few seconds later, shaking her gently to get her attention. Her eyes met his—a good sign—and her lips moved.

"I can't hear you," he shouted.

She shook her head and pointed to her ears.

"Oh. You can't hear me either." He pointed at the door, where Willis was poised to shoot at the first sign of a threat. "We have to go."

She nodded, seeming to understand, but then reached out and grabbed something off the floor beside her.

The tomahawk head.

Bones brought himself to one knee, then cautiously rose to his feet.

So far, so good. He extended a hand to Rose, helped her to her feet, and without letting go, led her toward the door, tapping Willis' shoulder to let him know they were ready to move out.

There was a body lying just beyond the entrance, a Caucasian man wearing a hoodie, splotched with blood from a pair of entry wounds in his chest, and still holding a silenced pistol in one outstretched hand. As they stepped past, Bones bent down, planning to help himself to the weapon, but Rose squeezed his hand to get his attention and shook her head. She lashed out with a foot, kicking the pistol, sending it skittering away across the carpeted floor. Then she grabbed Willis' hand, indicating that he should leave the other gun behind as well.

He stared at her like she was crazy, and said something, possibly to that effect.

Rose shouted something that was either an obscenity or *Trust me.*

Probably the latter.

Willis frowned, but then thumbed the magazine release and racked the slide to clear the chamber, before wiping the pistol down with the edge of his T-shirt and tossing it back into the office.

"Great," Bones muttered. "Now we're unarmed."

But just a few seconds later, he realized the wisdom of her decision.

Although he couldn't hear it, a fire alarm was blaring, probably triggered by the smoke from the flash-bang. Flashing strobe lights mounted high on the walls were showing the way to the fire stairs, and people were already streaming out of the other offices on the floor, heading for the exit. He assumed that they had all heard the noise of the grenade detonating, but not the subsequent shots. As far as anyone knew, it was a fire emergency, not an active shooter event, which would have necessitated a different, more defensive response—locking down the building and sheltering in place until the SWAT team arrived. If he and Willis—who were not only physically imposing, but conspicuously not white—were spotted running through the building with guns drawn, they probably wouldn't make it past the front door. Unarmed as they were, they could simply go with the flow.

That would get them out of the building at least, but if the two goons who had just tried to kill them had brought along reinforcements, they would be up the creek.

Hang on a sec, Bones thought. *What the hell just happened?*

While he was no stranger to life-and-death situations, he usually had some idea of who the bad guys were and what they wanted. This attack had come completely out of the blue.

Suppressed weapons. Flash-bang grenades. Military-grade hardware. Whomever their enemy was, they had access to some serious firepower, and they weren't afraid to use it in a crowded public place.

But who had they been targeting? And why?

This wouldn't be the first time that he stumbled into the middle of someone else's problem. Maybe Rose had pissed somebody off with one of her lesson plans. But the timing of the attack just didn't feel like a coincidence.

The tomahawk? He shook his head. *No. That's crazy.*

Even if the hatchet had belonged to the real Captain Falcon, at best, it was a collector's item. And who else besides them even knew of the discovery?

He would have posed the questions out loud, but since he wouldn't have been able to hear the answer, what was the point? If Rose knew the answers, she would tell them when they were safe— and able to talk with their inside voices. Until then, all that mattered was staying alive.

CHAPTER 7

Maddock's gag reflex jerked him back into reality, waking him into a nightmare of drowning. He thrashed about blindly, his body wracked with a coughing spasm as it tried to purge his lungs of the cold sea water. It took him a moment to realize that he was on the surface. It took a lot longer for him to remember where he had been before that.

He lifted his head out of the water and saw flames, scattered pools of oil and floating debris burning all around him, and realized intuitively what had happened.

The grenade he had tossed onto the rear deck had triggered a secondary explosion, probably the fuel tanks, and that had blown the cabin cruiser to smithereens. The blast had launched him out into open water.

His relief at having survived that catastrophe immediately gave way to panic. He dog-paddled in a circle, searching all around for *Sea Foam*.

"Maddock!"

The shout was faint but unmistakable. He spun around again, looking for the source of the voice, waving his arms above his head. "Corey! Here!"

A searchlight stabbed out through the gloom. Maddock oriented himself toward it and began swimming, but after a few seconds, the illuminated circle fell upon him, followed quickly by a ring lifesaver. He slipped one arm through the hole in the center and allowed his crewmate to reel him in like the catch of the day.

Corey still dressed in his bright orange survival suit and dripping wet from his own excursion, was alone at the other end of the rope.

"Where's Matt?" Maddock said as the other man reached down to pull him aboard.

"Out cold," Corey replied, nodding over his shoulder to an unmoving form sprawled on the deck.

"Shot?"

Corey shook his head. "I think he got hit by some flying debris. I made sure he was alive and breathing. Then I started looking for you."

"Any survivors on their side?"

"I didn't see anyone else. I think all that gear they were wearing probably dragged them down. Boss, what the hell happened?"

"We got lucky." Maddock looked out over the water again. "This time."

The damage to *Sea Foam* was mostly cosmetic and all above the water-line. Matt Barnaby on the other hand probably had a concussion, but even if his injuries had not been serious enough to warrant medical attention, Maddock's decision to return to port would have remained unchanged.

Although piracy on the high seas was becoming increasingly common, Maddock was fairly certain that the men who had attacked them had not been mere brigands attempting to seize a target of opportunity. They had been speaking English, with American accents, and their weapons and equipment marked them as professionals—paramilitaries or mercenaries.

A hit squad.

But working for whom?

Until he had an answer to that question, the search for the *Waratah* would have to be put on hold.

The sat phone started ringing when they were still fifty miles from port. It was Bones.

"You're not gonna believe what happened to us."

Maddock felt his pulse quicken. "Let me guess. Someone tried to kill you."

There was a long silence on the line—the unavoidable delay of satellite transmission lag—and then he heard Bones say. "Dude, you told him?"

Willis's voice was barely audible. "When would I have done that? We've been together the whole time."

"Just tell me what happened," Maddock said.

He listened patiently as Bones recounted everything that had transpired, beginning with their meeting at the Buffalo University and ending with their narrow escape from the two gunmen.

"We had some unexpected company here, too," Maddock said when his partner finished.

"That proves it then. They're going after everyone who knows that we found Falcon's tomahawk."

Maddock frowned. "Bones you know how I feel about coincidences, but honestly, I can't see how an old axe head rates attention from an international hit team."

"The tomahawk is just the tip of the iceberg. Rose can explain it better than me. I'll let her tell you when we get there."

"Wait, you're coming here? Are you sure that's a good idea?"

"Positive," Bones said. "If she's right, that's where the answers are."

"You mean the wreck?"

The lag delay was maddening, but not as maddening as Bones' cryptic answer. "Not exactly."

"Antarctica?" Maddock glanced over at Bones, and then back to Rose Greer. "You're serious?"

The red-haired woman nodded confidently. "That's where Captain Falcon found it."

"The Outpost?"

"That's what my great-granddad called it in his book."

They were gathered in the restaurant of the Durban hotel where Maddock and the others were checked in under assumed names. Despite a killer headache and a new scar, Matt had declared himself fit for duty, but Maddock thought it best to steer clear of *Sea Foam* for a while.

"I read the book on the flight over," Bones supplied. "It matches exactly what we found. The clipper, the second airplane and the mid-air collision. Even the hatchet was right where the book said it would be. It all fits."

Maddock made a mental note to add *In the Shadow of Falcon's Wings* to his already out of control To-Be-Read list, even though he was pretty sure Rose had already hit all the salient points.

As she told it, in 1938 or thereabouts, a young pulp fiction author named David "Dodge" Dalton had gone looking for Falcon—the man who had inspired his fictional stories—after the kidnapping of the American president. That daring crime had been committed by a gang of mercenaries using technology that, even in the present sounded like it belonged in a Buck Rogers story—exoskeletons made of an indestructible metal that imbued the wearer with, among other things, the power of flight and the ability to shoot lightning bolts. Over the course of the novel, it was revealed that the exoskeletons were actually the creation of an advanced early human civilization—artifacts discovered by the "real" Captain Falcon in an ancient outpost buried under the ice at the bottom of the world. Dodge pursued the president's kidnappers literally to the ends of the earth, and after escaping the Outpost—which actually seemed to be some kind of elaborate prison facility—chased after the kidnappers' plane—a stolen prototype for the Boeing 314—in a smaller floatplane—a bi-wing Grumman J2F "Duck." In the climax of the story, the two planes collided in mid-air, and were last seen plummeting from the sky as the heroes escaped using some of the advanced Outpost technology.

All except for Captain Falcon, who made the ultimate heroic sacrifice.

"Think about it," Bones continued, enthusiastically. "There's no way the government would have let a story like that go public. A kidnapped president. The theft of an advanced aircraft. Lightning weapons. They had to cover it up. Then and now."

Maddock raised a skeptical eyebrow. "You think our government sent those killers after us?"

"Not the whole government. You know how it works. One hand doesn't know what the other is doing. Plausible deniability. We're probably dealing with some kind of black-budget defense research agency. They've probably been exploiting the tech from the Outpost for the last eighty years."

Maddock frowned. "If any of that were true, why would they have let this Dodge Dalton write his book in the first place?"

"Because, without tangible evidence—like that plane—it reads like science fiction. You try to suppress that, it just makes people suspicious."

"Actually," Rose added, "the story was only published a few years ago. Maybe it went out before they could stop it, and they've been watching to see if anyone would take it seriously."

Bones turned to Rose. "Tell him the rest."

"There's more?" Maddock said.

Rose grinned sheepishly. "It's more conjecture than proof, but… Mr. Maddock, have you ever heard of Station 211?"

"Sounds like the name of a ska band."

"It's actually the name of a facility rumored to have been built by the Nazis in 1939, in Neuschwabenland or New Swabia, a territory in the region of Antarctica known as Queen Maud Land. It's about 2,600 miles south of here."

Maddock nodded slowly. "Nazis."

"Station 211 is just a rumor, but a Nazi expedition to Antarctica really happened in 1938. The area was officially a Norwegian territory, but that didn't stop the Nazis from moving in. The purpose of the expedition was ostensibly to create a whaling outpost for Germany. Whale oil was still an important resource at the time, but the explorers spent the better part of two years flying over the interior, surveying it and, according to some reports, finding ice free areas in the Mühlig-Hofmann Mountains, fertile green valleys fed by hot springs. In the more outlandish stories, they found technology from the ancient civilization of Atlantis."

Maddock exchanged a look with Bones.

"I know," Rose went on, misinterpreting the look. "It sounds crazy. But after the war, Admiral Richard Byrd put together a huge expedition—Operation High Jump—to explore the same area. Byrd reported finding a green valley with forests growing on the surrounding slopes. Even stranger, in an interview Byrd warned of an unspecified threat from aircraft based in the polar region."

"He actually used the words 'flying objects,'" Bones chimed in. "A lot of people believe that Operation High Jump was actually a mission to retrieve alien spaceships originally discovered by the Nazis."

Maddock knew that his partner loved a good conspiracy theory, especially when aliens were involved.

"Another popular theory was that Byrd was speculating about the possibility of a hollow earth, with entrances at the poles. That's also something the Nazis believed." Rose raised her hands in a defensive gesture. "I'm not saying I believe any of that, but it's a well-known fact that the American government scooped up a lot of Nazi scientists after the war."

"Operation Paperclip," Bones supplied.

"Admiral Byrd might have been acting on secret information about Nazi activities in Antarctica."

"So you think this Station 211 is the Outpost described in your grandfather's book."

"Great-grandfather, but yes. I mean, until you guys showed up, I didn't think any of it was real, but…" She shrugged and looked over at Bones. "Like he said. It all fits."

Maddock wondered if Bones and Rose were being a little too hasty in pinning everything on a grand conspiracy, but he was having trouble coming up with a plausible alternative. Complicating the situation was the fact that Jimmy Letson had gone off the grid. That wasn't like Jimmy, and it had Maddock more than a little worried.

If the government really was willing to kill them to cover something up, then there was only one way to take the heat off.

Expose it for everyone to see.

"Okay," he said. "Pack your long johns. We're going south."

CHAPTER 8

Maddock had a rough idea of the challenges they would face below the Antarctic Circle, but the first major obstacle presented itself before they could even depart. Just getting to Antarctica would be a prodigious undertaking.

At her maximum sustainable cruising speed, it would take *Sea Foam* five days to reach the coast of Antarctica, a voyage that would take her through some of the most dangerous seas on the planet. But even if the yacht had been built to withstand the harsh polar environment, there was another far more compelling reason not to travel by water. *Sea Foam* had already been attacked only 200 miles from port. Maddock doubted they would survive a second attack, especially if it happened 2,000 miles from civilization. Flying in was a much better option, but unfortunately it was almost prohibitively expensive.

Almost.

For the low price of just $20,000, a Cape Town-based logistics agency provided round-trip air passage to Novolazareskaya, a Russian research base situated on the Lazarev Ice Shelf. In addition to being a hub for scientific pursuits, "Novo Base" provided a staging area for thrill-seekers and adventure tourists, the kind with more money than sense.

Maddock secured passage for himself, Bones and Rose—the rest of the crew would stay in Durban with *Sea Foam*, to hopefully leave a blind trail for the hit squad to follow—and after dropping a few more bills on polar equipment, the three of them boarded the plane, a massive Russian-made Ilyushin Il-76, painted white with a bright blue nose and a stripe running down the length of the fuselage, for the six hour flight to the end of the earth.

"This little jaunt is going to put a dent in our rainy day fund," Maddock said.

"What good is having a platinum card if you can't splurge once in a while?" Bones replied. "Besides, if we don't come up with something to get those goons off our backs permanently, all the money in the world isn't going to make much difference."

"True enough. Which brings us to the question of where we go once we get there." He turned to Rose. "Any idea where we're supposed to look for this Station 211?"

"If that was known, it wouldn't be a rumor anymore. It's generally believed that Admiral Byrd found what he was looking for in the Mühlig-Hofmann Mountains, but you won't read that in the official sources. It's the same reason why you won't see it on Google Earth."

"I see why you and Bones get along so well. How

did Dodge Dalton find the Outpost?"

"The devices from the Outpost react with each other. Sort of a magnetic attraction. They're drawn to it like a homing beacon. It's something to do with the metal. A scientist my great-granddad worked with called it 'adamantine.'"

"Like in the comic books?" Bones said.

"Greek mythology, actually. It was the indestructible metal of the gods. The chains of Prometheus were forged from it."

"Unfortunately, we seem to be fresh out of ancient adamantine gizmos," Maddock said. "Unless you've been holding out on us."

"Actually, I think we do have something." She dipped into her shoulder bag and brought out the tomahawk head.

Bones folded his arms over his chest. "The aliens made that?"

"They weren't aliens, Bones," Rose replied patiently. "And no they didn't, but I think it's possible that it may have picked up some of the properties of adamantine."

"Sort of like magnetizing a piece of steel," Maddock said. "That could explain why it doesn't show any sign of corrosion. You think that will be enough to guide us?"

"I was thinking we could suspend it on a string, like a pendulum or dowsing rod. Once we get close to the mountains, we should observe some kind of effect." Rose gave a helpless shrug. "I hope. Sorry. It's the best I've got."

Maddock just nodded.

It was a balmy 31 degrees Fahrenheit on Schirmacher Oasis, the ice-free plateau where Novo Base, with its three-mile-long airstrip was situated. Rose, with her heavy parka tied around her waist, and her polar-fleece jacket liner unzipped, strolled down the plane's cargo ramp like it was a summer day—which in fact, it was. She stretched after the long flight and took in a deep breath. "Wow. Africa and Antarctica in the same day. Now I can cross them both off my bucket list."

Bones, fully-outfitted in his cold-weather clothes, was less enthusiastic. "I could have gone my whole life without coming here. Remind me again why I'm here instead of Matt? Rangers love this cold weather crap."

"You mean aside from his concussion?"

Bones made a dismissive gesture. "Pshaw. I had a flash-bang blow up in my face. I still can't hear out of my left ear."

"Okay. Then how about the fact that we might just be about to crack one of the biggest UFO mysteries in history. Admit it. You wouldn't miss this for the world."

Bones gave a non-committal grunt. "I'm just saying, I wish it was a little warmer."

"This is warmer," Rose said. "You really should peel off some of those layers until we're out on the ice. You're going to perspire in there, and believe me, you don't want your sweat freezing."

"Oh, suddenly you're the polar expert?"

"I'm from Buffalo. I know a thing or two about cold weather."

"Keep your goggles on though," Maddock added. "Snow blindness is one of the biggest dangers of being here."

It would have been more accurate to say that snow blindness—literally sunburned eyeballs—was one of the *most common* dangers. The affliction, which caused symptoms ranging from a painful sensation—some described it as a feeling like having broken glass under the eyelids—to temporary loss of vision, was just one of a long list of hazards awaiting visitors to the southern ice, but unlike those others, it took a few hours of unprotected exposure to the glare of sunlight reflecting off the ice for the symptoms to set in. It was painful, but not immediately lethal, unlike most of the other items on that list.

Although there were limited guest facilities on the plateau, it seemed prudent to spend as little time there as possible, so as soon as their gear was off the plane and loaded onto a bright yellow snowcat—another service provided by the logistics company for a small fortune—they headed out.

In keeping with their cover story, they had submitted an itinerary for their "adventure ski vacation," but it had also seemed wise to avoid stating their actual destination, which meant that the weather report and crevasse map supplied by the logistics company were pretty much useless once they left the plateau. The only way to safely negotiate the various hazards of the landscape— weak ice-bridges over geothermal heated lakes and streams, crevasses that could swallow the snowcat whole—was by moving slowly and paying attention to tell-tale clues on the surface. The Mühlig-Hofmann Mountains were only about a hundred and twenty miles from Novo Base, but traveling in a straight line was out of the question, and what should have taken them four hours took closer to fourteen, or at least it felt that way.

Maddock was used to long hours of travel on the water, but driving the snowcat was nothing like putting *Sea Foam* on a heading and letting her do all the work. He had to be wide-awake and fully alert every second, even when he wasn't at the controls. After two hours, he switched out with Bones, and then Rose demanded a turn. Since the cab was heated and they had round the clock daylight it made sense to keep driving, but by the time they finally reached the figurative end of the road, they were almost too exhausted to set up camp.

Outside, they got a taste of what Antarctica really had to offer. Maddock and Bones had to fight a steady ten-mile-an-hour polar blast and sub-zero temperatures, but once the tent was pitched and anchored, the interior immediately began warming up thanks to constant sunlight bathing the exterior panels. With the last of their energy, they stripped down to their thermal underwear and crawled into their sleeping bags.

"Yes!"

Rose's shout roused Maddock from a deep dreamless sleep. He felt like he had only just drifted off but when he glanced at his watch, he saw that more than six hours had passed.

He sat up and looked over to see the historian bent over something on the floor of the tent, but looking at him with a triumphant grin. "It works," she said. "Check it out."

Maddock squirmed out of his warm sleeping bag and crawled over to her. When he saw what she was doing, he reached over and slugged Bones until the latter stirred.

Maddock ignored his friend's warning growl. "Wake up," he said. "You need to see this."

Rose had threaded a length of paracord through the axe eye—the slot where the wooden handle, or haft, was supposed to go—and was dangling the tomahawk head like a plumb bob.

Only it wasn't dangling. Not straight down at least. Instead, the cord was stretched taut at a shallow angle, just a few degrees below horizontal. Maddock reached out and touched a cautious finger to the metal blade. It was warmer than he expected, and swayed a little. He applied more pressure, pushing it down several inches, but when he moved his hand away, it fell—or rather rose—back to its previous position.

"Holy crap," Bones muttered, now fully awake. "That's trippy."

"Like I told you," Rose said. "We can follow it like a dowsing rod. This will take us right to the Outpost."

"In case you weren't paying attention today," Bones replied, "You can't always travel in a straight line down here. And we don't know if it's a mile or a hundred miles."

"I think there's a way to narrow it down a little," Maddock said, pulling on his snow pants.

Once they were suited up, they all headed out into the biting cold. The hatchet head continued to hang askew, always pointing in the same direction no matter which way they turned. Maddock oriented his GPS unit—unlike the sat phone, which relied on communications satellites, the global positioning system was truly "global" in its coverage—and stared toward the mountain peaks in the distance.

He plotted the azimuth into the GPS, then they started off on foot, heading away from it and the shelter of their camp, at a perpendicular angle to the invisible line for a distance of about a mile, and then plotted in another vector. The two lines crossed in a valley about twenty-five miles southwest of their camp. The elevation at the site was nearly two hundred meters higher than their present location, but the hatchet head was still pointing at a slight downward angle.

"It's under the ice," Bones said. "That's not going to make this easy."

"If you're right about Base 211, someone else may have already done all the hard work," Maddock replied. "I guess we'll know when we get there."

It took three hours to find a pass through the maze to the valley marked on the GPS. As they got closer, the "angle of the dangle" as Bones put it, increased but surprisingly even when they were squarely on the coordinates, it did not point straight down.

"I guess X doesn't mark the spot after all," Bones said.

"Maybe I was off by a couple degrees when I ran the plot," Maddock said. He doubted that was true, but couldn't think of a better answer.

"I don't think that's it," Rose said. She held the axe head out in front of her and turned her body until she was facing the same direction it was pointing. "I think we just need to keep following wherever it leads."

Maddock glanced over at Bones who was peering through the cab window. "I'm not sure we'll have to do that," he said, his enthusiasm finally breaking the grip of the cold. "I know where we need to go." He pointed toward a distant black peak protruding above the ice in the direction Rose was indicating.

"That mountain? You seeing something I'm not?"

"It's not a mountain," Bones said. "Look closer. It's a pyramid."

Maddock was not as certain about the identification as Bones. The jutting black massif did look perfectly symmetrical, with what looked about like the same angles as the Great Pyramid of Khufu on the Giza Plateau in Egypt, but he had seen plenty of similar rock formations carved by nature rather than the artifice of human engineers.

Man-made or not though, the axe head was leading them in that direction.

They drove the snowcat as close to it as the terrain would allow, and then debarked to finish the trek on foot. The slope was so steep that they had to break out the mountaineering equipment in order to keep going. The axe head continued to lead them forward even though, by climbing, they were almost certainly moving further and further away from whatever it was they were trying to find.

Then they found the cave.

CHAPTER 9

Maddock shone his flashlight into the icy throat, but beyond about twenty yards, the beam vanished into shadow, illuminating nothing.

He glanced over at Bones. "Something's not right about this."

They had ventured only a little ways inside, just far enough to find shelter from the constant wind, so he didn't have to shout to be heard, but even without the wind, it was brutally cold. The perpetual summer sun did not reach very far beyond the threshold of the ice cave.

"What are you talking about?" Rose interjected. She held out her hand, displaying the makeshift pendulum which was still pointing ever so slightly forward, into the depths of the ice tunnel. "The hatchet brought us here. This is exactly where we're supposed to be."

"We came here looking for a secret base, built by the Nazis and taken over by the U.S. government. Or whoever it was that tried to kill us. So where is it?"

Bones nodded slowly. "He's right. It doesn't look like anyone has been here in… forever."

Behind her goggles, Rose's eyes widened in surprise and alarm as she began inspecting the immediate area. "Maybe this is a back door. I don't know. But this *is* what we came here to find."

Maddock had no argument for that. "Maybe you're right. Watch your step and stay on your toes."

They started forward, down a smooth sloping passage that seemed too perfect to have been created by natural forces, but showed absolutely no indication of having been bored out by artificial means. The tunnel curved gently but relentlessly to the right, a counter-clockwise corkscrew spiraling down into the ancient ice. The grade was so steep that, without crampons and ice axes, they probably would have been unable to walk it, but as they made their way down, the dangling tomahawk head began to lift, indicating that their descent was indeed bringing them closer to the anomaly that was affecting the axe head.

After about fifteen minutes of trekking, the passage opened into a much larger cavern in the ice. The floor of the hollow was flat and clear. The walls were curved, like the inside of an enormous air bubble frozen in the ice, but cutting through the middle of the cavern was a slanted flat wall. The thin layer of clear ice could not hide the black stone underneath.

"The pyramid!" Bones said.

"We've been circling it," Maddock confirmed. "I'd guess we're about four hundred feet down from where we started."

Rose checked the tomahawk again. It was

hanging straight out in front of her. "We're almost there."

Almost where? Maddock wanted to ask, but the answer appeared as if by magic.

"That wasn't there a second ago," Bones said, pointing to a triangular opening in the stone wall.

Maddock was pretty sure it wasn't. "I guess this is where we need to go.

The tunnel, like the opening, was a perfect equilateral triangle, about nine feet high from base to apex. The black stone remained partially hidden under the ice, but the shape was unmistakable. A short ways in however, they reached a junction with a transverse passage.

"Decisions, decisions," Bones muttered. "Should we flip a coin?

"No need." Rose held out the cord attached to the axe head, but it continued to point straight forward, into the unyielding wall.

"So much for that idea. I've got a quarter in my pocket, but I can't get to it with all this stuff on. You want to reach in for me?" He winked at her.

Rose rolled her eyes. "Get Dane to do it."

"Let's try left," Maddock said, ignoring the banter.

"Why?"

"Why not? If it doesn't lead somewhere, we can always turn back and try the other way."

Bones looked at Rose and they both shrugged.

The passage extended for about thirty yards

before making a right turn. As they moved, the tomahawk shifted, relative to their direction of travel, but kept pointing to a fixed point somewhere on the other side of the wall until, midway down the adjacent passage, they came to another opening. The tomahawk was pointing straight into it.

Rose laughed nervously. "Wow. It feels like something's pulling on it."

Maddock looked over. The cord trailing from her hand was stretched taut. He reached out and put his hand on the cord, feeling the tension there. "May I?"

She looked back at him suspiciously, but then nodded.

He twisted the cord around his gloved hand once, twice and then gripped it firmly before telling her to let go.

He thought he was prepared for the transfer, but the cord almost yanked him off his feet. He allowed himself to be drawn forward, his curiosity more powerful than his caution. Just beyond the entrance, the passage opened into an enormous vaulted chamber—the hollow interior of the pyramid.

Bones looked up in awe. "I'll bet this was some kind of hangar. For the UFOs."

Maddock glanced over at Rose. "I thought this place was supposed to be some kind of prison. Wasn't that what you're great-grandfather's book said?"

Rose shook her head uncertainly. "Yes, but in his next book, the Outpost was destroyed, so I really don't know how reliable they are."

"There's a second book?"

"Actually, there was a whole series. You can buy them online."

"That would have been good to know earlier." Maddock shot an accusatory glance at Bones.

The latter shrugged. "I didn't know."

Maddock continued forward, following the tomahawk like someone being pulled along by an enormous dog straining against its leash, until it crunched into an enormous ice hummock. Although his light could not reach to the lofty apex, Maddock had no doubt he was standing almost directly beneath it, and that the goal of their search lay in the exact center of the structure.

"There's something hidden under here," he said. He let go of the cord and the tomahawk remained where it was, plastered against the hummock. He took out his mountaineering axe and began chipping away at the ice around the object, but after just a few hits, the jagged pick end broke through, revealing an empty space at the center. Even stranger, when he wrestled the pick free, a puff of warm air hit his face. He took another whack at it, and this time, a section of ice bigger than his head broke loose and vanished into the newly created hole, along with the tomahawk.

Maddock shone his light into the gap and saw, just a few feet away, a black sphere, about eighteen inches in diameter. Stuck to it like a paperclip to a magnet, was the tomahawk. The object was completely ice free, and suspended in mid-air with no apparent means of support. The small cavity inside the hummock was thick with a strange fog, like dry ice vapors, leading Maddock to believe that the object was somehow sublimating the ice— evaporating it without first melting it into water— and freeing itself after years, or perhaps even millennia, of imprisonment.

"I think we woke something up," he said, not looking back. "Bones, give me a hand with this."

The big man stepped forward and added his ice axe to the effort, and in a matter of minutes they hacked out an opening large enough to crawl through. Maddock shouldered his way into the gap. The air inside was warm, but only in comparison to the sub-zero conditions outside. Maddock felt no radiant heat from the object.

He wormed in a little further, until he was close enough to touch it, which he did after only a moment's hesitation. He knew there was a faint possibility that he would get fried to a crisp like a fly in a bug-zapper, but his instincts told him that if the object—the artifact or orb or whatever it was—was dangerous, it was probably already too late.

The object bobbed a little at his touch but that was all that happened.

He gripped the cord attached to the tomahawk, and gave it an experimental tug. The orb moved toward him like a helium balloon on a string, but as he pulled it closer, he could feel the resistance increasing, as if the black sphere was being pulled back to its original position by an invisible bungee cord. He pulled harder still, wrestling the orb out of the cavity in the hummock, and wrapped both arms around it to keep it from going anywhere.

Bones let out a low whistle. "Holy crap. What the hell is that thing?"

"I don't know, but I'm guessing it's the reason those goons tried to kill us."

"Goons, Mr. Maddock?" The unfamiliar voice echoed in the vast hall. "That's unkind."

Adrenaline dumped into Maddock's bloodstream as he whirled around, shining his light at the perimeter of the chamber, searching for the source of the voice. Bones grabbed Rose, thrusting her behind him, as if to shield her with his body, and shone his light out as well.

As if in answer, several spots of light appeared near the entrance; high-intensity LED lights, all trained on the three of them.

"I'm sure if you really got to know us," the voice went on, "You would come up with something much more colorful."

CHAPTER 10

The lights grew brighter as the men holding them moved closer. Maddock squinted against their brilliance but did not look away. He counted six lights in all. Bones shone his own light at them, revealing what Maddock already knew in his gut: the lights were attached to the Picatinny rails of assault rifles. The weapons were wrapped in white camouflage tape, and the men carrying them wore similarly colorless winter coveralls, with matching ski masks and gloves. There was a seventh man in the center of the formation, similarly attired, but without weapon or light. They stopped about ten yards from Maddock and the others, spread out in a semi-circle with their weapons all raised and ready.

"Drop the light, Mr. Bonebrake," the unarmed man said. "And raise your hands, all of you."

It was the same voice that had addressed them from the darkness. His face was completely concealed behind a white scarf and goggles.

"Who the hell are you guys," Bones said, his voice almost a snarl. He lowered the light but did not comply with the other demands. Maddock likewise remained exactly as he was, clutching the orb in a bear hug.

The man laughed without humor. "When I said you should get to know me, I was being facetious.

TBH, it would be a waste of time for both of us."

"Then why haven't you just killed us," Maddock said. "Maybe you're afraid of what I can do with this?"

He thrust the orb forward, and was pleased to see several of the gunmen flinch. It was worth the effort of manhandling the sphere, which wobbled in his grasp like a living thing, struggling to break free and return to where he had found it. Only his firm grip on the tomahawk head kept it from doing so.

The man composed himself and managed another laugh. "I could ask you the same question, but then I already know the answer. You have no idea what it is you've found. No idea of its potential. Or how to unlock it."

"Wrong," Rose said. It came out as a hoarse, fearful whisper, but she cleared her throat, straightened and took a deep breath. "You're wrong about that. My great-grandfather literally wrote the book on this place, and I've read every word. If you don't back off, I'll show you just how much I do know."

Despite the gravity of their situation, Maddock felt a swell of pride for Rose's courage in facing down their foes.

The other man cocked his head sideways to look at her. "Ah, Ms. Greer. Yes, I'm familiar with those books. Very entertaining science fiction, but hardly what I would call a user's manual. If you're clinging to the hope that you will be able to use the anomaly against us as a weapon, I fear you will know only disappointment before you die."

Maddock didn't know if Rose was bluffing, but the fact that the man was still talking told Maddock that *he* was. And just like that, the pieces fell into place.

"You didn't know how to find this place, did you?" The silence that followed confirmed Maddock's guess. He pushed forward. "All this time, we thought you were trying to cover this up, but you were looking for it, too."

"And you led us right to it," the man replied. "Bravo, Mr. Maddock. You are as good as your reputation."

"Crap," muttered Bones, then looked up suddenly. "Wait. So are you or aren't you working for the government?"

The man ignored the question. "Cards on the table, Mr. Maddock. I don't think you know what to do with the anomaly, but I have no idea what will happen if I try to kill you while you are holding it. I'm prepared to take that chance, but all things being equal, I'd just as soon not. So, in the interest of expediting things, I'll be generous. Put it down, right now, and I will allow the three of you to leave."

"Uh, huh," Bones said. "Sure you will."

The man spread his hands in mock-apology. "I tried. Though, TBH, I would have been disappointed if you had said 'yes.'"

"TBH? Seriously, dude. WTF? Do you have any idea how stupid that sounds?" Bones turned his gaze to the other gunmen. "Have you told him how stupid that sounds?" He shook his head and added, "SMH."

The commando leader ignored him, and turned to the gunman on his immediate right. "Try not to hit the anomaly."

"Wait!" Maddock shouted.

The other man held up a hand, signaling his minions to stand fast. He cocked his head at Maddock. "You're full of surprises. Or is this where you try to lull me into complacency and then at the last second…what's the expression? Pull a fast one?"

Maddock shrugged, careful not to lose his grip on the sphere. "You've got all the guns."

"Yes, I do. You would do well to remember that, Very well, then. Put it down and walk away."

Maddock slowly, carefully, pushed the orb away from his body, holding it out in both hands. "Come and get it."

"Dude," Bones muttered in a low voice. "This isn't usually how we do things."

Maddock looked his friend in the eye. "It's the only way, Bones. Just be ready to move as soon as I hand it over." He let his gaze flick ever so slightly to the right, hoping that Bones would get the message

Bones nodded slowly.

The leader of the commando team—Maddock decided to call him "TBH"—turned to his chief lieutenant again. "If anyone of them so much as sneezes…"

The gunman nodded and squared his shoulders

behind the stock of his assault rifle, making sure that the barrel was pointed straight at Maddock.

TBH advanced with slow tentative steps, until he was standing only a couple feet away. He cautiously reached out for the orb.

"Careful," Maddock warned, just before contact was made. The man flinched as if he had been stung, which was exactly the reaction Maddock had been hoping for. He grinned. "This thing has a mind of its own. You sure you really want it?"

TBH sneered through the scarf covering his face, and then closed his arms around the sphere.

Hidden from the other man's view, Maddock tightened his grip on the tomahawk head and braced himself for what he knew was coming. "All yours, then."

He let his other hand drop and stepped to the side, wrenching the tomahawk loose even as the orb yanked the other man forward toward the center of the pyramid. Unbalanced, TBH lurched forward, stumbling as he tried to stay on his feet while being dragged along.

In the split-second that followed, as the gunmen struggled to process what they had just seen, both Bones and Maddock sprang toward them, with Bones rushing the men on the right and Maddock running at the men on the left. The high-intensity tactical lights flashed as the men tried to reacquire the moving targets, but before they could, the two former-SEALs had tackled two of the six gunmen to the icy floor.

Although the commandos had superior numbers and firepower, Maddock and Bones had just turned those advantages into liabilities. The gunmen couldn't shoot at them for fear of hitting one of their own comrades, which bought the two treasure hunters a few seconds to figure what to do next.

Bones squirmed around behind the commando he was fighting and then reached out with his long arms to grab the man's assault rifle by the stock and barrel. He pulled it up as if curling a barbell, level with where he thought the man's throat might be, and then jerked back hard, crushing the receiver assembly into the man's windpipe.

Maddock's solution was quicker and more decisive. He slammed his fist—the one holding the tomahawk—into the side of his foe's head. Although the heavy hood of the man's white parka muted the sound of the impact, it offered little protection from blunt force trauma. The man went limp, dazed, unconscious or possibly dead. Still clutching the axe head, Maddock snatched up the man's rifle and squeezed the trigger.

A deafening report filled the chamber. Maddock hadn't really taken the time to aim, and none of the rounds found their mark, but the eruption of noise and the random impact of bullets against inward sloping walls triggered a hailstorm of ice fragments. The remaining gunmen scattered, sprinting for cover behind the hummock.

"Rose!" Maddock shouted. "Run for it!"

Before she could move however, a fierce shout rose from the center of the hummock. Maddock brought his captured rifle around, shining the tac-light on the commando leader who was now standing without difficulty, gripping the orb in both hands. Even from several yards away, Maddock could tell that something was different. The air seemed to be vibrating, crackling with something like static electricity.

A cold knot of dread seized Maddock's guts. Without hesitating, he pulled the trigger, emptying the rifle's magazine at the standing figure, but instead of spattering the ice behind TBH with bloody chunks of flesh, the bullets evaporated with little blue flashes, right in front of the man.

The commando leader never even flinched.

The rifle went silent, its ammunition gone, but through the ringing memory of the thunderous reports, Maddock could hear laughter.

"Well what do you know?" the man chortled. "The anomaly creates an impenetrable energy shield, just like in the Dodge Dalton book. Let's see what else he got right?"

Then, the orb in his hands began to crackle and dance with long fingers of blue-white lightning.

CHAPTER 11

Maddock knew he wouldn't be able to outrun the lightning, so he did the only other thing he could think to do. Tossing the empty rifle aside, he drew back his arm and hurled the tomahawk.

He didn't aim it at TBH, but instead launched it over his foe's head.

The other man, perhaps confident in his invincibility or lost in his apotheosis was oblivious to the piece of steel whirling above his head. It arced around like a boomerang, and then shot toward him like a guided missile. The energy shield might have protected him from bullets, but the adamantine-infused tomahawk passed right through, seeking out the orb.

There was a bright flash and a pop, like a light bulb burning out, and then darkness.

Half-blinded by the abrupt shift from brilliant light to gloom, Maddock blundered forward, rushing to the barely visible figure slumped on the ground in front of the hummock. TBH lay face down, his body covering the sphere. Because of his white camouflage outerwear, it was difficult to distinguish him from the surrounding ice, but the red stain between his shoulder blades was unmistakable.

Maddock knelt and rolled the man onto his side.

The metal sphere shifted with him, as if pinned to his body, which was exactly what had happened. The tomahawk head, drawn by the energy field of the orb, had effortlessly passed through both the energy shield and the commando leader, killing him instantly. The spike on the back of the axe blade had penetrated clear through the man and now protruded from his chest to make contact with the orb.

There was something different about the sphere, though it took Maddock a moment to realize what had changed. The orb was no longer being drawn toward the center of the pyramid. Whatever the commando leader had done to activate it had evidently switched off its automatic homing function.

What the hell is this thing?

"Maddock!" Bones yelled from behind him. "Time to go!"

As if to underscore the urgency of the admonition, a burst of rifle fire ripped through the air in the chamber, followed by several more.

Maddock knew they would never make it to the exit, not unless he came up with a major game changer.

"Really wish I'd read that book," he muttered as he reached out for the orb. He braced himself, expecting a shock or worse, but the only unusual thing he felt was a slight warmth radiating from the metal, penetrating the thick fabric of his gloves. He tried to lift it but encountered resistance from the body of TBH, which was still pinned to the sphere. He got it free, but only after planting his feet against the man's torso and pushed with all his might until the axe head tore loose.

He turned the orb in his hands, looking for a switch or control panel, but the metal was smooth, a perfect sphere without any disruptions. "Power on," he shouted. "Shields up."

"Don't say it!" Rose called out, her voice barely audible over the din. "Think it!"

Think it? Maddock shook his head, and then did just that, mentally uttering the same commands.

Nothing changed. *But if it did,* he thought, *would I even know it?*

He imagined an invisible barrier, a bubble of energy around him, like something from a science fiction movie, stopping the bullets cold.

He had no idea if it was really there at all.

He turned to find Rose and Bones a few steps away. The latter was firing his captured assault rifle to keep the remaining enemy pinned down, but Maddock knew he would soon run out of ammunition.

"Bones! I'll cover you. Go! Now!"

Bones gave him a sharp, doubtful look, but then grabbed Rose by the hand, and started across the icy floor toward the outer edge of the chamber. Maddock sprinted after them. The points of his crampons scraped uncertainly on the floor. The climbing spikes were designed for slow deliberate movement, not running, but he stayed on his feet. Directly ahead, searching beams of light cast a shadow-show on the walls of the chamber, accompanied a moment later by the thunderous reports of multiple assault rifles. Maddock expected at any moment to feel the hammer-punch of a bullet, or worse, to see Bones or Rose struck down, but miraculously, they all reached the triangular passage unscathed. Either the orb was truly shielding them or they were just that lucky.

Bones led the way, navigating the passages back to the exterior with uncanny precision. As they emerged out into the ice cave, they found a pair of unusual vehicles—they looked like a cross between amusement park bumper cars and fan boats—waiting just outside the entrance.

Bones shook his head. "I guess now we know how those jokers managed to get down here so fast."

"What are those?" Rose asked.

"Hovercraft," Maddock said, approaching one of the sleek vehicles. Its white fiberglass upper hull rested on an air skirt that looked like an enormous inner tube. The open cockpit had a control console at the front, with a long padded bench running lengthwise down the middle. The controls were basic, not much different than a jet ski, with a set of handlebars, a bank of indicator dials and a key in the ignition. He grinned in satisfaction. "And it's our express ride out of here."

"You know how to drive it?"

"How hard can it be?" Maddock dropped the orb into the foot well, and then clambered over, straddling the bench behind the console. He turned the key and hit the ignition switch, and was rewarded with a faint hum as the fan assembly at the rear began spinning. The machine was a lot quieter than Maddock expected. During their time in the SEALs, he and Bones had ridden on large military air-cushioned landing craft, big enough to transport Humvees from ship-to-shore. Those sounded a little like the inside of a tornado, but this was barely louder than a lawn mower. As the rushing air pressurized the flexible skirt, the hovercraft began to drift a little. Maddock experimented with the controls and quickly figured out how to more or less make the machine do what he wanted it to.

"All aboard!"

Rose hesitated, so Bones swept her up in his arms and deposited her in the back of the idling craft, but instead of immediately following her, he moved over to the second hovercraft and used his ice axe to tear a large gash in the rubber air skirt.

"That should slow them down a few minutes," he shouted as he climbed over.

Maddock nodded and turned the nose of the craft toward the mouth of the cave, and goosed the throttle. The hovercraft slid across the ice, picking up speed as it shot into the narrow passage.

"Who were those guys?" Rose shouted.

"No clue," Maddock replied, not looking back.

"But I don't think they're working for the government."

"Then who?"

"You think it could be our old pals?" Bones said.

Maddock shrugged. "Could be."

"Who are you talking about?" Rose said.

"A bunch of racist nutjobs that call themselves The Dominion," Bones explained. "We've tangled with them before. This is just their style."

Maddock knew the far-right quasi-religious terrorist group did not have an exclusive on turning ancient relics of power into weapons of destruction, but he did not contradict his friend. "As soon as we can get a call out, we're gonna drop this hot potato in Tam's lap."

"Who's Tam?"

"A lady we work for sometimes. She *does* work for the government."

"You trust her?"

Bones just laughed. He and Maddock had an unusual relationship with Tam Broderick, the leader of a CIA task force called "the Myrmidons," dedicated to squashing the Dominion permanently. Maddock and Bones occasionally freelanced for her, but when it came to trust, they knew that Tam could be trusted, first and foremost, to do whatever it took to accomplish the mission.

After a few scrapes and bumps, Maddock got the hang of driving, and opened the throttle to full, pushing the hovercraft up the slope like a rocket. It had taken them fifteen minutes to descend the corkscrewing passage, but less than five minutes after leaving the cavern at the base of the pyramid, a light appeared at the end of the tunnel. Maddock didn't slow down.

"Hang on!"

The hovercraft raced toward the opening and then shot like a bullet from the mouth of the ice cave.

Rose's screams seemed to echo across the valley, but after just a few seconds, what had been a shriek of terror changed to a whoop of exhilaration as the hovercraft slid down the side of the ice-covered pyramid like a runaway roller coaster.

Maddock allowed himself a grin of triumph, but as the valley floor rushed up at him, his sense of elation fizzled like a dud firecracker.

At first, he thought his eyes were playing tricks on him. Aside from their waiting snowcat, the landscape was a uniform white, but as they got closer, he saw that it was no mirage.

Surrounding the snowcat, barely distinguishable from the sparkling white ice, were four more camouflaged hovercraft.

CHAPTER 12

The wind whipping through the open interior was bitterly cold, cutting through Maddock's scarf and face mask like they were made of cheesecloth., but he gritted his teeth against the frigid blast and gripped the handlebars like they were the only thing keeping him from flying off into oblivion. As the valley floor loomed closer, he could just make out the human figures crowding around the idle vehicles. He didn't need to see the men clearly to know that they were probably packing some serious firepower.

Maddock figured they had one thing going for them: the commandos below didn't know what had happened inside the ice-bound pyramid, and had no idea who was in the hovercraft racing down the slope toward them. That uncertainty would only last until the gunmen realized that the trio were wearing North Face parkas instead of white camouflage shells.

"Stay down," he called back to the others. "We're going to blow through."

He would have preferred to veer off, skirt the valley floor and keep as much distance between them and the commandos as possible, but on the steep downslope, the idea that he was in control of the hovercraft was just wishful thinking.

The slope flattened out and he felt the craft decelerating. Now he could see the other hovercraft clearly, silhouetted against the horizon ahead, and right in front of him, the snowcat, with its heater and all their gear and food, seductively close, impossibly out of reach.

He pushed the throttle to its maximum and steered away from it. In the corner of his eye he saw movement, commandos jumping out of their motionless hovercraft... Pointing... Shouting....

Shooting.

With a loud crack, the fiberglass hull to Maddock's left erupted in a spray of splinters. Almost simultaneously a second crack—the sharp report of an assault rifle—echoed across the valley.

Maddock cut right, or tried to. Steering a hovercraft was accomplished by turning the control vanes on the fan, redirecting the flow of air at an angle, but the machine had a lot of forward momentum to overcome. It behaved more like a hockey puck than an ice skate. Instead of changing direction, the craft started to spin on its axis, turning dizzying curlicues across the icefield as it continued more or less in the same direction. He quickly corrected his mistake, pointing the nose in the direction of travel.

A few more shots were fired but none of them found their mark, and after a few more seconds, they ceased altogether. A quick backward glance revealed why.

The commandos were in pursuit.

Maddock reckoned they had about a three-hundred-yard lead on the enemy hovercraft, easily within the effective range of their assault rifles. They had not started firing yet, but it was only a matter of time before the lead started flying again, and any attempt at evasive maneuvers would only shrink the distance between them. He kept the throttle maxed, but knew he would never be able to outrun a bullet.

"Rose!" he shouted without looking back. "If you know how to make that orb work for us, now would be a really good time."

"I'm trying!" she replied.

Maddock wondered if that was the explanation for how they had made it through the gauntlet relatively unscathed.

Bones leaned over his shoulder, shouting in his ear. "Hope you've got a back-up plan, dude."

"Working on it," Maddock answered. He checked the fuel gauge. The tank was three-quarters full, but he had no idea how far they could get on that. Novo Base was at least a hundred-and-fifty miles. The coast was a lot closer, but neither option would necessarily mean safe harbor if the commandos decided to chase them all the way.

And if they couldn't make it that far, it probably wouldn't matter. They would freeze to death at the bottom of the world.

It felt like a replay of the showdown on the open ocean. Outnumbered and outgunned. Nowhere to hide and no chance of outrunning their enemies. That left only one option.

Déjà vu all over again, he thought.

"I've got an idea," he said, and then added. "You're not gonna like it."

Bones clapped him on the shoulder. "As long as it's not turning around and playing chicken with these guys, count me in."

Maddock grimaced behind his scarf. "Umm…."

"Crap. You're kidding. That's your plan? What are we gonna do, throw snowballs at 'em?"

Maddock looked over his shoulder to where Rose was kneeling in the bilge space, hugging the orb. "Rose! How's that force field coming?"

She looked up and gave a helpless shrug.

Bones heaved a sigh. "Okay, let's do this."

Maddock nodded and gripped the handlebars. "Hang on!"

He cut hard to the right and, as before, the hovercraft pirouetted, turning around without immediately changing direction. Just as quickly, he straightened the control vanes, stopping the spin at the halfway point so that they were sliding backward. The machine shuddered as momentum fought a losing battle against the air being forced through the fans. The hovercraft slowed, stopped for just an instant, and then began moving forward, back into the valley.

The four enemy hovercraft seemed to be moving across the ice at warp speed, a hundred… seventy-five yards away, side-by-side in a picket line. Orange-yellow tongues of flame lanced out from the approaching vehicles. They were so close now that, even if he had wanted to, Maddock couldn't have veered off to avoid a collision.

"Hang on!" he shouted, and then there was a lurch as the hovercraft rose up beneath him and went airborne. The sensation abruptly changed to a feeling of weightlessness as the craft fell away, but that too lasted only an instant. The hovercraft crashed down, bouncing and skipping across the ice.

Maddock struggled to get upright again. The hovercraft seemed intact. He could only surmise that it had somehow—impossibly—ridden up and over the other machines.

Had Rose succeeded in using the orb to create a protective force field around them?

He glanced back, saw both Rose and Bones, hanging on for dear life, apparently unhurt.

The valley floor ahead looked clear, but unfortunately, the only way out of it was up the steep slope of a mountain. He knew the hovercraft could make the climb—the commandos had done it when they had followed them into the ice tunnel—but it would be slow going and burn a lot of fuel.

Then something happened that sent a chill down Maddock's already freezing spine.

Appearing as if from nowhere, rising above the black pyramid, was an enormous airplane. It had the same profile as the Il-76 that had borne them across the Southern Ocean—wide fuselage, shoulder wing configuration with four engine nacelles and rear stabilizer wings mounted atop the elevated rudder, but unlike that jet, this aircraft was a dull battleship gray. The plane swooped down, filling the valley with its bulk, and then just like that, it was above them, passing so close that Maddock ducked reflexively. He glanced up quickly, saw that the plane's landing gear was fully deployed, its rear-cargo ramp already lowered.

The plane was going to land. The bad guys had called for reinforcements.

Crap. Maddock thought. *As if things weren't already bad enough.*

Bones was shouting something, but the roar of the jet's engines drowned him out.

He glanced back, ready with a shout of his own. "Rose! If you've figured out how to control that thing, now would be—"

The rest of his sentence was lost in a new eruption of noise—not the distinctive report of assault rifles but something much louder, a rapid staccato burst, like a string of firecrackers amplified ten thousand times.

Directly behind them, a second sun—a white-hot supernova—blossomed into existence.

Maddock instantly knew what had happened, and when he spun the hovercraft into another 180° to get a look, his suspicions were confirmed.

A giant plume of ice marked the spot where the giant jet aircraft had just touched down, but the space between them and it had been transformed into a battlefield of fire and ice.

Bones let out a whoop of triumph. "Holy crap, dude. Did you see that?"

Maddock nodded dumbly.

Amidst the geyser-like steam plumes rising from flash melted ice were a dozen smaller fires sending up columns of black smoke—the burning wreckage of at least one of the hovercraft, and the smoldering bodies of the gunmen who had been riding in it, scattered haphazardly across the ice.

As the jet had passed over them, its anti-missile countermeasures had been activated. The magnesium flares, which deployed in a shotgun burst, were a defensive measure, designed to fool a heat-seeking missile by providing it with a thermal target even hotter than the plane's engines, but someone onboard the aircraft had used them as a weapon against the commandos.

"That was a C-17," Bones continued. "An Air Force bird. I never thought I'd say it, but hooray for the cavalry."

Maddock scanned the terrain ahead. The plane—a C-17 Globemaster, if Bones' identification was correct—had stirred up a blizzard of swirling ice and smoke, but at the periphery of the storm, he saw something moving away at a right angle.

At least one of the commando hovercraft had survived.

"Save the celebration until we're clear," Maddock said. He opened the throttle wide and the hovercraft charged forward.

As they neared the artificial ice storm, Maddock saw the commando hovercraft turning, coming around to pursue them. In the corner of his eye, he spotted another machine on the opposite side, likewise maneuvering for another attack, and then the world dissolved into a haze of blowing ice.

The hovercraft crunched and shimmied through the flaming debris, but after a few seconds, the cloud thinned enough for him to see the C-17, its engines still blasting out roiling convection waves of heat exhaust. The ramp to the open cargo hold beckoned invitingly, as did the two figures standing on it, arms waving in a "hurry up" gesture.

Over the roar of the jet engines, he could just make out the sharp crack of rifle fire. The figures on the ramp reacted. One of them ducked back inside the plane, the other produced a handgun and began firing back.

Maddock kept the throttle maxed, closing the remaining distance in seconds to race up the ramp, past the man who was still firing his pistol at the pursuing commandos, and into the cavernous cargo bay.

It was like being swallowed by some monstrous leviathan.

He reversed the throttle, but the craft had too much momentum to simply stop. Thankfully, the cargo space was empty. He caught a glimpse of some moving in front of him, scrambling to get out of the way, but then the forward bulkhead filled his vision and he barely had time to brace for the imminent collision.

The crash wasn't as bad as he expected. The hovercraft had already given up most of its forward velocity, but the sudden stop nevertheless ejected him from the machine, hurling him into the bulkhead. His winter clothing afforded him some protection, but the impact knocked the wind out of him.

For several seconds, all he could do was lie stunned and motionless on the deck. He could hear shouting voices, and then felt a shudder rising through the deck plates as the aircraft began moving... accelerating.

The plane was taking off.

All he could do was hang on as the aircraft surged forward, the deck tilting upward as the plane climbed back into the sky. When it finally leveled off, he sat up.

Bones and Rose were gingerly climbing out of the hovercraft, the latter still holding the mysterious orb. Behind them, at the far end of the long tunnel-like cargo bay, the ramp was rising. Maddock caught a final glimpse of the ice-covered valley and the distinctive black pyramid before the door closed, sealing them inside the belly of the beast.

They had made it. They were safe.

EPILOGUE

The man who had fired the pistol from the ramp walked calmly up the length of the cargo bay toward them. The second figure, the one that had nearly been run down, was also advancing and as he approached, he pushed back his hood and removed a full-face ski mask, unleashing a long cascade of black hair.

"He" was actually a she, and Maddock recognized her instantly.

Bones spoke first, his voice evincing the same disbelief that Maddock felt. "Jade?"

Jade Ihara, the half-Japanese, half-Hawaiian archaeologist, who happened to be Dane Maddock's ex-girlfriend, offered a half-smile. "That was quite an entrance."

"Jade." Maddock pulled the scarf away from his face. "What the hell are you doing here?"

"I was in the neighborhood. Lucky for you."

"Never thought I'd say this," Bones chortled. "But damn it's good to see you." He looked past her to the other man. "Prof, is that you?"

Pete Chapman, who had earned the nickname "Professor," had served with Maddock and Bones when they were SEALs, and was currently working with Jade as a facilitator and sometimes-bodyguard, though his actual employer was the U.S.

government, and specifically, Tam Broderick's Myrmidons task force.

But the man walking toward them stripped off his cold-weather covering, revealing medium-length wavy dark hair, a full beard, and an unfamiliar face.

"Actually," Jade said, "Pete's off doing a favor for Tam. So are we, I suppose. She's the one who put us on your trail."

Maddock frowned. He was starting to remember why Jade was his ex-girlfriend. "Who's 'us,' Jade? You obviously know a lot more about what's going on than I do."

"For a change," Jade shot back.

"Is there something going on between you two?" asked the bearded man.

Bones laughed. "Duh."

Maddock ignored him and faced the stranger. "Maybe you're who I should be talking to."

"Probably." The man looked past him to Rose and the black metal sphere in her arms. His eyes widened in surprise. "You found it?"

"You know what that thing is?" Bones asked.

"Not really. I know that they call it 'the anomaly,' but not much more than that."

"But you know who 'they' are?" Maddock said. "The guys that just tried to kill us…The Dominion?"

The man shook his head. "They call themselves 'Prometheus.' They're very secretive, and very powerful."

Bones snorted. "Great. Just what we needed. It's

like we got put on some kind of mailing list for Villain-of-the-Month Club."

"What do they want?" Maddock pressed.

"What everyone with power wants; more power. They want to rule the world. And they want control of things like that." He pointed at the orb. "Unfortunately, that's about all I can tell you about them, and I've been hunting them for twenty-five years."

"Since kindergarten then?" Bones said. It wasn't much of an exaggeration. Beneath his beard, the man looked like he might be in his early thirties.

"It's a long story," the man replied.

"I'm guessing you've got a few of those," Maddock said. "You got a name?"

The man stuck out his hand. "Nick Kismet."

Bones laughed again. "Is that like, your stage name?"

Jade rolled her eyes. "Way to call the kettle black, *Bonebrake*."

Kismet laughed, too. "That's another one of those long stories. Actually, I work for a UN cultural preservation agency. My job is to protect antiquities. Keep them out of the hands of people like Prometheus."

Maddock nodded in Rose's direction. "So you're here for that? The anomaly. Take it. It's all yours."

Kismet and Jade exchanged a look, then the latter spoke. "Maddock, the anomaly is just the—"

"Don't say it," Bones cut in.

"—tip of the iceberg," Jade finished.

"She said it," Bones groaned.

"It's true, Mr. Maddock," Kismet confirmed. "Prometheus has begun their endgame, and it's up to us to stop them. All of us. This is just the beginning."

The End

For more Dodge Dalton, enjoy this preview of

AT THE OUTPOST OF FATE
A DODGE DALTON ADVENTURE

"Gosh. What happened next? How ever did you escape?"

David Dalton — "Dodge" to both his intimate friends and the thousands of Americans who eagerly devoured his Sunday syndicated feature "The Adventures of Captain Falcon" — glanced over at the breathless young woman and the man with whom she was conversing, curious to see how the question would be answered.

The mountainous hulk that was "Hurricane" Hurley shifted nervously in his chair and averted his gaze, glancing down at the newspaper clenched in his massive paws. He had been reading aloud the latest installment of Falcon's adventures — as one of Captain Falcon's trusted confidants during the Great War, he was not only a contributor to the ongoing serial, but also a key player — eager to impress his pretty young blonde tablemate with this most recent tale of derring-do.

It wasn't at all like Hurricane to be caught with nothing to say. Dodge considered letting the big fellow suffer a little longer, but then decided to affect a rescue worthy of Falcon's chronicler. "Sorry miss," he interjected, gesturing with his champagne flute, "but you'll have to wait a week like everyone else."

The blonde girl's lips turned down in a pout, but Hurricane seized the opportunity and recovered his composure. "We had been in situations a good deal worse than that. I remember the time Jocasta Palmer nearly drowned us in fish eggs."

Dodge smiled absently and took a sip of the bubbly, letting his attention wander. He felt partly responsible for Hurley's embarrassment. In the past year, the Falcon adventures had relied less heavily upon the historical account inarticulately recorded in Hurricane's unpublished — some would say 'unpublishable' — memoirs, and more on Dodge's own imagination. Hurley had not objected; the Falcon stories had never been more popular, and ostensibly as the only member of Falcon's coterie of heroes still in circulation, he was more than happy to be the sole focus of attention at sporting events, county fairs and other public gatherings frequented by attractive, starstruck young ladies. Unfortunately, the hero of the story didn't have a clue about how some of these latest adventures would end.

Dodge didn't feel too guilty over taking creative control of the serial. It wasn't like he was rewriting history. Hurley's magnum opus read exactly like what it was; a pulp adventure worthy of the Sunday comics. While the man was certainly an imposing physical presence, and had probably served with distinction in the Great War, the outlandish exploits of Captain Zane Falcon, Father Nathan Hobbs and Brian "Hurricane" Hurley were simply too unbelievable to be anything but fiction.

It had been pure serendipity that Dodge, a sportswriter for The Clarion, had been buttonholed by an editor too intimidated by Hurley to say no, and given the task of cleaning up the meandering prose for publication. In only a few short months, "The Adventures of Captain Falcon" six column inches times two, and a single cartoon illustration — also Dodge's work — had been picked up by King Features and now ran in every major Sunday newspaper in the country. Now, three years later and at the height of their popularity, all of Hurley's stories had been told. The well had dried up, and it was up to Dodge to fill the void, which he had done admirably, boosting readership to a new peak. All of which had brought him here, to a garden party in the most famous garden in America.

"Another glass, sir?" inquired a voice at his shoulder.

He glanced up at the nattily attired waiter, but before he could answer in the affirmative, a ripple of anxiety passed through the group of diners and people began rising to their feet. He shrugged apologetically and stood up just as the band launched into the customary ruffles and flourishes. Dodge craned his head to get a look at the man who was both host and guest of honor but couldn't see him through the crowd. Abandoning the effort, he simply followed the example of everyone else, standing at attention until the final note was played. He applauded along with the rest of the crowd and then queued up in the orderly reception line as the band segued from "Hail to the Chief" into "Stars and Stripes Forever."

Perhaps because he felt more dread than anticipation for the impending introduction, the time spent waiting flew by quickly, and in a matter of only minutes he heard a voice made familiar by weekly radio discourses speaking his name... well, almost. "Mr. Dodge, isn't it?

It was a common mistake. "Dodge" was a nickname the sandy-haired athletically inclined writer had earned during a boyhood summer spent running bats out to the on-deck circle at Ebbets Field. Normally, he would have gently corrected the error, but this time he thought better of it.

"That's right, Mr. President." He shook the extended hand, mildly surprised to see the chief executive of the country seated behind a small café table.

"That's a good firm grip you've got there," observed the President. "You must get your exercise."

"I played a lot of ball as a boy, sir."

"Aha. And do you tag along with Falcon and his team on their adventures?"

Dodge forced a chuckle. "Only in my daydreams. I fight Falcon's villains with the pen, not the sword."

"I'm a big fan," the President announced with

what appeared to be sincere joviality. "Big fan. Can't wait to see how Falcon gets out his latest scrape. Keep up the good work, young man. You're a national treasure."

Dodge correctly read the exit cue and moved on, letting the Commander-in-Chief have the final word. He strode away, but not before he heard: "Hurricane Hurley! Why, you're even more impressive that I had imagined. How did you get so strong?"

The walking mountain gave a thunderous guffaw to the delight of everyone in line. Even Dodge couldn't resist a smile as he heard Hurley, with the barest of prompting, launch into an elaborate anecdote about his childhood on the Cumberland Plateau.

He and Hurley had become friends after a fashion, and while the six-and-a-half foot giant wouldn't have been his first choice for company on a Friday night, there was no denying that an aura of rough charm surrounded the man they called Hurricane. Part of that was most certainly his proclivity for exaggeration, which had played no small part in the creation of the Captain Falcon legend. Dodge had heard this particular tall tale before and knew it always grew with the telling. Leaving Hurley to his admirers, he went in search of the waiter with the champagne service.

To his chagrin, he found that the beyond the reception line, the party seemed to have ground to a halt. Instead of the gentle rumble of multiple conversations, there was only a faint hum of awed whispers. The attention of the group, more than three score in number, was fixed skyward. Movie stars stood alongside cocktail servers, gaping in consternation at what appeared to be a flock of birds around a distant airship. Curious, he joined the stilled crowd. "What's all the fuss?"

"Barnstormers," suggested one man. "Some kind of aerial circus."

Frowning, Dodge looked again, squinting into the mid-morning sun. The array was much nearer than he had first realized and steadily moving closer. He now saw that what he had first taken to be birds were in fact... "Those are men up there."

"Parachutists," ventured the man.

"There aren't any parachutes," argued one woman. "But they aren't falling; they're flying!"

Dodge verified her statement with a glance, then looked to the airship at the center of the formation, thinking perhaps that the men were suspended by fine wires. What he saw however only further confounded a logical explanation.

The aircraft, if it was indeed that, was like nothing he had ever seen, save perhaps in dime novel artwork. The vessel looked like a round cake pan and was just as featureless. There appeared to be no means of propulsion — no spinning propellers or rocket flames — yet it was moving far too rapidly to be a dirigible carried on the wind. One thing was certain however: the aerial display was moving inexorably toward the White House.

"I'll wager this is something the Army cooked up; some new secret flying machine. The President probably arranged this stunt as entertainment for the party."

There was little conviction in the tone of the man voicing this opinion. It sounded more like an unsuccessful attempt to hide growing panic. Dodge's gut reaction was similar; something bad was about to happen. "I think we should take cover."

It was as though a dam had broken. In an instant, the quiet group of onlookers became a pandemonium of shrieks and frantic purposeless running. Dodge was buffeted by the human tide, and then just as suddenly found himself standing alone near the perimeter of the garden. After the chaos of the fleeing mob, the ensuing quiet was eerily peaceful.

Then the sky fell.

The next moment was surreal; something glimpsed in a dream or spawned from his pen in the latest chapter of Falcon's adventures. An invisible hand slapped him against the perfectly manicured lawn. He had only a dull memory of the collision; it felt something like a belly flop dive into a warm swimming pool, rather than a forceful trauma such as might accompany being struck by a solid object. He lingered there, pressed to the ground by a blanket of pressure that seemed everywhere all at once.

"Hellfire!" Hurricane's voice thundered above

the din, but any further imprecations were lost in a deafening hail of gunfire.

In the corner of his vision, Dodge could just make out a contingent of dark-suited men — the President's Secret Service bodyguards — forming a skirmish line. Their backs were to him, their faces set against the entrance to the West Wing, which was the only means of egress from the Rose Garden, and each man's Thompson sub-machine gun spat a lethal volley of lead at the unseen attackers.

Then a different noise split through the chaos. It was a crack like the discharge of a pistol, but louder in volume and longer in duration. There was a blinding flash of light and when his ability to see returned, Dodge saw a break in the line. One of the Secret Service men had been pitched backward several yards and lay motionless with wisps of smoke trailing from his scorched clothing. However, Dodge's gaze was riveted elsewhere, for through the gap in the wall of bodyguards, he got his first good look at the party crashers.

They were men, the same men that had flown apparently unaided through the skies, but men nonetheless. The one who now blocked the President's only avenue of escape wore no particular uniform, but the singular distinctive accessory to his ensemble defied simple explanation. At first glance, it looked like some kind of medical apparatus or perhaps a medieval torture device. A framework of metal rods outlined the man, reaching down from a rigid waist belt to hinged footpads, up to his shoulders and down the length of his arms, and finally connecting to a domed cap, like something worn by medieval infantrymen. The rods were jointed at the elbows and knees to allow fully articulated movement, but where hands ought to have been, Dodge saw what looked like heavy armored gauntlets. The intruder brandished these metallic fists at the Secret Servicemen, disdaining the muzzle flashes of his foes' guns. Without warning, another brilliant flash arced through the air and blasted a second bodyguard from the line.

Dodge realized two things in that instant: First, that the blinding discharge could only be lightning —artificial lightning from a cathode in the attacker's heavy gauntlets; and second, that the man wearing the strange exoskeleton seemed to be impervious to bullets.

One by one, the Secret Servicemen were scattered like so much chaff by the unknown enemies' lightning bolts. There were at least half a dozen of the intruders, all wearing the metal gloves that shot electricity and all apparently invulnerable to any sort of counterattack.

Suddenly a new combatant appeared on the field of battle; a giant warrior who eschewed firearms and weapons in favor of the equipment Mother Nature had bestowed. Hurricane Hurley, roaring like an enraged grizzly bear, waded into the fray swinging his fists like war hammers. One of the intruders bounced away from a blow as if imprisoned in a giant beach ball. Two more were slapped aside as indifferently as buzzing flies; evidently the invisible armor that deflected bullets was no match for the human touch.

As the tide began to turn, it occurred to Dodge that he had not moved since the attackers' untimely arrival. When he tried to rise however, he again felt the insistent pressure at his back, like an enormous rubber balloon filled with water. As he pushed harder, the opposing force grew, then just as abruptly vanished. He craned his head around to get a look at the cause of his temporary immobilization.

He digested what he saw in large chunks of incredulity. The first thing he noticed was an expanse of dull silvery metal looming overhead and eclipsing the sky; it could only be the airship he had glimpsed from afar. The craft was almost close enough to touch, at least fifty feet in diameter, and its surface was impossibly smooth, without and seams or rivets. Yet all of those observations paled when held against the next thing Dodge ascertained about the invaders' aircraft: it was floating.

Except floating wasn't exactly the right word. It didn't bob or waver like a moored dirigible or hovering gyrocopter; rather it was absolutely motionless, as though the whole thing were the roof of a building supported on invisible columns. Momentarily overcome by journalistic curiosity, he reached up to touch the smooth underbelly of the craft, but the artificial thunder of the invaders' weapons snapped him back into the moment.

Hurricane stood transfixed in the path of a sizzling lightning bolt. Astonishingly, the giant was not blasted aside as the President's guards had been. His normally curly black hair stood straight up and his jaws were clenched, teeth bared in a rictus of pain, but he did not budge; he was as immovable as the airship. The tendril of electricity continued to lick at his torso a moment longer, then winked out. Dodge surmised that the weapon employed some sort of capacitor and that it had entirely expended its stored charge. Hurley shook his head, shrugging off the assault like a prizefighter, and charged at the now impotent attacker.

Lightning flared again, not from the man on the ground, but from the floating disc. Hurricane staggered back as the discharge struck him in the chest, but he recovered in an instant and renewed his advance. Another blast, this time a sustained tongue of sizzling blue fire, and then a second. To Dodge's utter amazement, four more intruders, all wearing metal exoskeletons, descended from the airship on a ramp that had deployed unnoticed from its underbelly. The reinforcements concentrated their electrical weapons on that lone target, and even the prodigious Hurricane Hurley could not endure such a withering assault. As the juggernaut went down, the clamor of combat immediately ceased. A few Secret Servicemen remained upright, but had discarded their useless weapons in order to create a defensive ring around the man they were sworn to protect. It was a futile gesture. The intruders, ten altogether, advanced menacingly and peeled the bodyguards away to reveal the object of their quest: the President of the United States.

The Chief Executive sat motionless at his table, his gaze locked warily on the man directly before him. His lips were pursed tight; if he said anything in defiance of the assault, or heaven forbid, begged for mercy, it was spoken too softly to be heard by anyone but those who now held his fate in their hands. Two of the men seized hold of his arms and bodily lifted him away from the table. The President was again lost from view as the remaining attackers formed a perimeter around their prize and commenced escorting him to the idle airship.

Dodge remained where he was, paralyzed with fear and disbelief as the Commander in Chief was taken up the ramp into the hovering craft. It was simply too much to absorb; anonymous commandos equipped with exoskeletons that imbued their wearers with the powers of flight and invincibility, shooting bolts of lightning and kidnapping the President. It was like....

"Like something from a Falcon story," he whispered. But Falcon wouldn't be frozen in place, petrified with fright as the foes absconded victorious. Falcon would take action! He would....

What would Falcon do?

Four of the invaders, along with their captive, entered the disc after which the ramp vanished back into the craft. The silvery metal skin sealed over the opening so that it was impossible to tell where the entryway had been. Then, without any sort of preamble, the airship leaped into the sky. Dodge felt a push, similar to what one might experience when a descending elevator car halted abruptly, but that was all. Whatever force motivated the craft, it seemed to operate in defiance of Newton's Laws.

The six remaining raiders formed a circle on the lawn, their steel gauntlets extended toward the defenseless guests that huddled for cover throughout the garden. One of them stood only a few paces from Dodge, so close that he could see the man's dark brown eyes and the rivulets of sweat that beaded on his forehead and trickled along a furrowed scar that ran the length of his jaw. The hard man locked eyes with Dodge and flashed a menacing grin. The meaning was explicit: stay back or get fried.

"Move out!" shouted another of the invaders, and then acting on his own admonition, he flexed his knees as if preparing to jump and was whisked into the sky. Another followed on his heels, zooming into the air as if there were rockets on his back. There were no rockets, only a metal lump, of the same dull color as the airship, which extended from the rigid belt of the exoskeleton up across the man's back. The scarred man threw Dodge a smug nod, then bent his knees in preparation to take flight.

Something broke inside Dodge. A sound, intimately familiar, but at the same time completely foreign, broke the ominous quiet. It was his own voice, and his words, while simple and ambiguous, felt like a declaration of war. He looked the man in the eye and in a grinding whisper said: "I don't think so."

Dodge had only one thought: seize the man to prevent him from escaping. Beyond that, he had only the vaguest idea of what might occur. Perhaps the police would be able to identify the culprit and compel him to betray his confederates... perhaps he could be used as a bargaining piece against the President's safety. He didn't explore all the possibilities; his attention was focused on the sole objective of restraining the man. In the instant before the man burst into flight, Dodge hurled himself forward and wrapped both arms around the intruder's waist. His momentum should have taken both of them down in a typical flying tackle, but what happened next was anything but typical.

As his arms opened around the man, Dodge again felt the same subtle pressure that had flattened him beneath the airship. He recognized it now or at least was able to reconcile it with a known phenomenon. The closest likeness he could come up with was the effect of magnetic repulsion; two magnets, lined up a certain way, would push each other apart. But the strange corona of force around the men had proven capable of repelling bullets — lead slugs with no magnetic characteristics — and even human flesh. Dodge could think of only one explanation, and it wasn't something he had read or heard about in the annals of science. Rather, it was the stuff of science fiction. The serials that shared the comics page with Falcon were always describing invisible force fields that could protect spaceships or superheroes. Dodge had always dismissed such stories as too fanciful to warrant serious consideration, but then again, he would have felt the same way about steel mitts that shot lightning bolts.

Whatever the cause, the energy field almost thwarted Dodge's desperate attempt to restrain the escaping rogue; his arms couldn't quite close together. He redoubled his efforts, hugging tightly to the shielded figure, but it was like trying to wrestle a greased pig. The force field seemed to squirm and ooze in his grip and for a fleeting second, Dodge knew he would fail. Then without any particular climax, the struggle ended and Dodge's arms locked around the man's metal shod ankles.

"Gotcha!" The momentum of his intended tackle maneuver had been lost, but Dodge had a taste of victory now. He tried to plant his feet, throwing his body weight to the side; but his shoes couldn't find the ground. His legs thrashed about, trying to somehow gain a position of advantage, but terra firma eluded him. He didn't have to look down for an explanation — somehow he knew with sickening certainty what had happened — but he looked anyway.

ABOUT THE AUTHORS

David Wood is the USA Today bestselling author of the action-adventure series, The Dane Maddock Adventures, and many other works. He also writes fantasy under his David Debord pen name. When not writing, he hosts the Wood on Words podcast. David and his family live in Santa Fe, New Mexico. Visit him online at davidwoodweb.com.

Sean Ellis has authored and co-authored more than two dozen action-adventure novels, including the Nick Kismet adventures, the Jack Sigler/Chess Team series with Jeremy Robinson, and the Jade Ihara adventures with David Wood. He served with the Army National Guard in Afghanistan, and has a Bachelor of Science degree in Natural Resources Policy from Oregon State University. Sean is also a member of the International Thriller Writers organization. He currently resides in Arizona, where he divides his time between writing, adventure sports, and trying to figure out how to save the world. Learn more about Sean at seanellisauthor.com.